Enid Blyton

MAGICAL FAIRY TALES

Look out for all of these enchanting story collections

by *Enid Blyton*

Enid Blyton

MAGICAL FAIRY TALES

hodder

HODDER CHILDREN'S BOOKS

This collection first published in Great Britain in 2020
by Hodder & Stoughton

1 3 5 7 9 10 8 6 4 2

Enid Blyton ® and Enid Blyton's signature are registered trade marks
of Hodder & Stoughton Limited
Text © 2020 Hodder & Stoughton Limited
Illustrations © 2020 Hodder & Stoughton Limited

A CIP catalogue record for this book is available from the British Library.

ISBN 978 1 444 95426 5

Printed and bound in Great Britain by Clays Ltd, Elcograf S.p.A.

The paper and board used in this book are made from
wood from responsible sources.

MIX
Paper from
responsible sources
FSC® C104740

Hodder Children's Books
An imprint of Hachette Children's Group
Part of Hodder & Stoughton
Carmelite House
50 Victoria Embankment
London EC4Y 0DZ

An Hachette UK Company
www.hachette.co.uk
www.hachettechildrens.co.uk

Contents

Mr Wumble and
the Dragon

Mr Wumble and the Dragon

MR WUMBLE was sitting in front of his fire, reading a book of fairy tales. When he read a story about a fierce dragon with fire pouring out of his nose he turned pale, and his hair stood up on end. When he came to where the prince rescued the princess from the fierce dragon he cried tears of joy. Then he read how the prince married the princess and lived happily ever after, and he was so pleased that he danced a little jig round the room.

'Oh, how I wish that I could have an adventure!' cried Mr Wumble, feeling sorry for himself.

'Mr Wumble, you forget yourself!' said his parrot.

He could only say three things, and that was one of them. Mrs Wumble had taught him to say them so that when she was away the parrot could remind Mr Wumble to behave himself.

Mr Wumble threw his spectacle case at the parrot, but it missed him and crashed into a vase that broke into more than a hundred pieces.

'Mr Wumble, I'm surprised at you,' the parrot said. That was the second thing it could say.

Mr Wumble stared at the broken glass in dismay. He didn't dare to think what Mrs Wumble would say to him when she came home.

'I'm going out,' said Mr Wumble, making up his mind very quickly. 'I'm going to have an adventure!'

'Have you got your handkerchief, your hat, your umbrella, your cough lozenges and your scarf?' said the parrot.

That was the third thing Mrs Wumble had taught him to say, because Mr Wumble had a bad habit of going out without putting on his hat and scarf, and coming back with a bad cold.

'Be quiet, you silly, stupid, ridiculous bird!' Mr Wumble said fiercely, putting on his hat.

'Mr Wumble, you forget yourself,' said the parrot in a very haughty tone.

Mr Wumble found his handkerchief, his hat, his umbrella and his cough lozenges. Then he tied his scarf round his neck.

'You can tell Mrs Wumble that I'm going out to look for an adventure,' he said to the parrot. 'I'm tired of sitting at home being poor good-for-nothing Mr Wumble! I'm going out to rescue princesses and fight fierce dragons!'

'Mr Wumble, I'm surprised at you!' said the parrot. Then Mr Wumble walked out of the front door.

He went out into the fields, looking for adventure as hard as he could. He looked in the hedges and in the ditches, but nothing happened at all except that his umbrella got caught in a hedge and he slipped into a ditch up to his knees.

'This is not a good day for an adventure!' Mr Wumble said to himself sadly.

Just at that very moment he caught sight of an aeroplane swooping down towards him. It looked exactly as if it was going to land on him. Mr Wumble turned and ran for his life, but he tripped over a stone and fell flat on his face.

Bump-bump-bump! The aeroplane landed just beside Mr Wumble, and someone jumped out and ran over to him.

'Have you hurt yourself?' asked the aeroplane man.

'Of course I have,' Mr Wumble said crossly. 'What do you want to go chasing me like that for?'

Mr Wumble stood up and looked haughtily down at the aeroplane man, who was very small with a very long nose. Mr Wumble wasn't a big man, and he felt quite pleased to be talking to someone smaller than himself for a change.

'I wasn't chasing you,' the aeroplane man said humbly. 'I was just going to ask you for some help.'

'Well, I'm rather busy at the moment,' said Mr Wumble, trying to sound important. 'Busy looking for a princess to rescue or a dragon to fight actually!'

'How marvellous!' said the aeroplane man. 'I was trying to find my way to Fairyland to find a prince. There's a wretched dragon worrying the princess of Silver River, and she sent me to find someone to rescue her. But now you can do it instead!'

'Jumping weasels!' said Mr Wumble, who often said strange things when he was surprised. Here was his adventure all right, but now he had found it he felt a little afraid.

'Well ... er ... um ... Is it a big dragon?' asked Mr Wumble nervously.

'Enormous!' said the aeroplane man. 'Hop in and I'll take you to the princess. She will tell you the whole story.'

Now Mr Wumble didn't mind going to Fairyland, but he certainly wasn't going to fight an enormous dragon. In fact, he thought that Mrs Wumble would be better at it than he would.

Still, he didn't like to seem a coward, so he said nothing more and soon found himself flying high over the town where he lived, on his way to meet the princess of Silver River.

'But at least I am having an adventure,' he said to himself. 'Just wait until I tell Mrs Wumble about this!'

'Mr Wumble, I'm surprised at you,' said a voice just by his ear.

Mr Wumble was so astonished that he nearly fell out of the aeroplane. He turned to see who had spoken, and there was his parrot sitting on the wing of the aeroplane, scratching its head with one of its feet.

Mr Wumble looked at the parrot in dismay. 'Oh, go away, you interfering, interrupting, inconvenient bird!' he said.

He gave the parrot a push, and it went over the side of the aeroplane. Mr Wumble leant over to look where it went, and forgot to hold on to his hat, which flew away behind him.

'Drat that niggledy, naggledy, annoying bird!' he said. 'It's made me lose my hat.'

'Mr Wumble, you forget yourself,' said a voice behind him.

Mr Wumble gave such a jump that the aeroplane wobbled from side to side. He looked round and saw the parrot was back again and, what's more, it held his hat in its feet.

'Snorting pigs!' cried Mr Wumble. 'There's my hat!'

He took his hat from the parrot and put it on again, just in time for the plane to land.

'Here we are,' said the aeroplane man.

The aeroplane was going downwards in circles, and when Mr Wumble looked out, he could see a large and glittering palace just beneath them.

'Bouncing bunnies!' exclaimed Mr Wumble in great excitement. 'A real, live palace!'

'Mr Wumble, you forget yourself,' said the parrot.

But Mr Wumble did not hear. He was far too busy feeling excited. Just think, he might soon be seeing a princess!

The aeroplane glided down on to the grass in front of the palace and came to a standstill. The little man climbed out and helped Mr Wumble down. The parrot flew on to his shoulder and wouldn't get off. Mr Wumble picked up his umbrella and felt about to make sure that he had a clean handkerchief handy.

'Now I'm ready to see the princess,' he said.

The little man led him up some steps and they came into a large, high room, where a beautiful princess lay reading on a couch. She came to meet them and shook hands with Mr Wumble. He forgot whether he ought to bow or to curtsy, so he did both.

'And who is this?' asked the princess, smiling so sweetly that Mr Wumble couldn't take his eyes off her.

'This is the person I've brought along to kill the dragon,' explained the aeroplane man. He had taken off his baggy clothes now, and Mr Wumble saw that he was really a little gnome, with a very long, pointed nose.

'I see,' said the princess, smiling again. She looked so sweet that Mr Wumble decided he wouldn't tell her just yet that he wasn't going to go near any dragon, big or small.

'What's your name?' asked the princess.

'Wumble, Your Highness – Mr Wumble,' said Mr Wumble. 'I am very happy to meet you.'

'When would you like to go out and kill the dragon?' the princess asked sweetly. 'Before tea or after tea?'

'Er – after, I think,' said Mr Wumble.

'Mr Wumble, I'm surprised at you,' the parrot said loudly.

Mr Wumble went very red, for he knew he had told a story and he was afraid that the princess would find him out.

'What a darling, quaint bird!' said the princess, and

she actually stroked the parrot's feathers.

'I can't bear the bird myself,' said Mr Wumble.

'Mr Wumble, you forget yourself,' said the parrot, putting up the crest on his head very angrily.

'Oh, the pet!' cried the princess. 'Did you hear what it said?'

'I'm always hearing what it says,' answered Mr Wumble.

'Here's tea,' said the princess. 'I hope you're hungry. Come and sit down beside me.'

Mr Wumble didn't know whether to be glad or sorry that tea had come. He wanted to eat some of the cakes that were in front of him, but he didn't like to think about the dragon he was supposed to go out and kill directly afterwards. The aeroplane man came over and sat down to share the delicious tea with Mr Wumble and the princess.

There were six different kinds of cream cake, two sorts of jam, and strawberry ice cream to finish up with. Mr Wumble didn't feel in the least like killing dragons when he had finished.

'And now, what about the dragon?' the princess asked the aeroplane man. 'Perhaps you'd take Mr Wumble to the hill where it lives, Longnose?'

Longnose said he would and Mr Wumble began to feel even more uncomfortable.

'I don't like to trouble you,' said Mr Wumble. 'I'm sure I could go by myself if you told me where to go.' Of course, Mr Wumble was hoping that he might be able to run off and hide somewhere, if only they would let him go off by himself. But they wouldn't. The princess came with him as far as the gate, and told him she would take care of the parrot till he came back.

'And if you don't ever come back, I'll be very kind to the parrot, I promise you,' she said.

Mr Wumble swallowed hard.

'Have you got your handkerchief, your hat, your umbrella, your cough lozenges and your scarf?' the parrot said suddenly.

Mr Wumble felt about for his handkerchief and his cough lozenges, tied his scarf more tightly round his neck, and checked his umbrella.

'Come along, come along,' said the gnome. And with the princess waving them goodbye, they set off in search of the dragon.

'We shall soon be there,' said the gnome. 'I do hope you can kill this dragon. It can scorch you to a cinder if you're not careful, so you must look out for his fiery breath.'

'Jumping weasels!' said Mr Wumble, feeling very shaky about the knees.

'Mr Wumble, you surprise me,' said a voice, and there was the parrot flying just above them!

'Drat that meddlesome, miserable, muddling bird!' cried Mr Wumble. 'I can't get rid of it!'

The parrot settled on his shoulder, and Mr Wumble had to put up with it. They all went on till they came to a hill.

'There you are,' said the gnome, pointing to a

column of smoke that rose in the air halfway up. 'That's the dragon's breath. Come back to the palace when you've killed it.'

Longnose ran down the hill and left Mr Wumble and the parrot alone. Mr Wumble turned very pale and thought he would run down the hill too. Then he thought of the princess's smile, and suddenly he made up his mind to go and take a look at the dragon. Perhaps he could kill it somehow, but he'd have to look the other way if he did – Mr Wumble wasn't much good at killing anything.

He hadn't gone very far before he heard a most peculiar noise. It was rather like a horse's cough, but about twelve times louder. Mr Wumble stopped and listened. The noise kept on and on and on.

Sounds like a very, very bad cough, thought Mr Wumble. *I wonder who it is.*

He went on cautiously, peering round every tree to see if it was safe to go on. The noise grew louder and louder. Then he saw smoke rising above the trees.

'Snorting pigs!' said Mr Wumble in a whisper.

'Mr Wumble, you forget yourself,' said the parrot.

Mr Wumble shook his fist at the parrot, and then took a look round the tree he was hiding behind.

He saw a most amazing sight. There was a big fire in the middle of a clearing, and crouched over it was a miserable-looking dragon. He was shivering from his head to his tail, and was making the strange noise that Mr Wumble had heard on his way up the hill. It was a cough – a very bad cough. Mr Wumble felt quite sorry for him.

He looked at the dragon's nose. There was no smoke coming from it – only the smouldering fire sent a blue column above the trees. Mr Wumble heaved a sigh of relief. The dragon didn't really look so terrible after all.

'Eheu, eheu, eheu!' coughed the dragon.

Mr Wumble suddenly did a strange thing. He stepped forward, held out his box of cough lozenges, and offered them to the dragon.

'Please take one,' Mr Wumble said politely. 'They are very good for coughs.'

'Thank you,' said the dragon in a hoarse tone. He put out a clawed foot, neatly took a lozenge from the box and popped it into his mouth.

'It's very good,' said the dragon after a bit. 'I shall be sorry to eat you after your kindness.'

Mr Wumble sat down suddenly. He had been so interested in the dragon's cough that he had quite forgotten about being eaten. He felt very much upset.

'That's a nice way to repay me for my kindness,' he said. 'I came here to kill you, but instead I gave you a cough lozenge.'

'So you did,' said the dragon generously. 'Well, I won't eat you – as long as you give me all the rest of your cough lozenges.'

'Well, I want some for myself,' said Mr Wumble. 'I get a nasty little cough in the mornings, you know.'

'Give me half then,' said the dragon. 'Go on, or I'll eat you up.'

'You be quiet,' said Mr Wumble, jumping to his feet and lunging at the dragon with his umbrella.

The dragon gave a yell and leapt out of the way.

'Mr Wumble, I'm surprised at you,' said the parrot, which made the dragon look round in astonishment.

'How does that parrot know my name?' he asked.

'Your name? Whatever do you mean?' asked Mr Wumble in surprise.

'My name's Wumble,' answered the dragon. 'Wumble the dragon. And I'm sure I heard your parrot say, "Mr Wumble, I'm surprised at you".'

'Well, if that isn't a funny thing!' cried Mr Wumble. 'My name's Wumble too – Mr Wumble. We must be cousins or something. I can't possibly kill you now!'

'Nor can I eat you,' said the dragon. 'Let's sit down and have a talk instead.'

So Mr Wumble and the dragon sat down by the fire and talked. They told each other all their troubles, and got on very well indeed. The dragon told Mr Wumble that he was very absent-minded, and because

18

he was always going out without his hat and scarf, he got dreadful colds. Mr Wumble said that he was just the same.

'But at least your parrot reminds you not to be forgetful,' said the dragon.

'And so does Mrs Wumble,' said Mr Wumble.

'Well, what do you want a parrot for as well?' the dragon asked in astonishment.

'I don't,' replied Mr Wumble, shaking his head gloomily. 'Mrs Wumble is quite enough.'

'Would you give me your parrot then?' asked the dragon eagerly. 'It would be so nice to have something that called me Mr Wumble, and reminded me of all the things I forget.'

Mr Wumble thought for a moment. Then he suddenly had a splendid idea.

'I'll give you my parrot and half my cough lozenges if you'll do something for me,' he said.

'Oh, anything, anything,' said the dragon.

'Well, look here,' said Mr Wumble, 'I've always

wanted to be brave and splendid – but somehow I've never been able to, and Mrs Wumble scolds me dreadfully. Now, if she thought that I had really fought and conquered a dragon – don't take offence now – she would be so astonished that she probably wouldn't dare to say another cross word to me ever again. If I could get her here somehow – I expect the princess could manage it – and you'd let me pretend to fight you, Mrs Wumble would think I was the bravest, strongest man in all the world.'

'No, I don't want to,' said the dragon. 'I don't like the idea of you fighting me. You might get excited and forget and stick a sword into me or something.'

'No, I promise I wouldn't,' said Mr Wumble. 'Do be a sport, Dragon. I'll give you my parrot and all my cough lozenges, if you like – but do say you will.'

'Oh, all right,' said the dragon. 'We'll meet at the bottom of the hill tomorrow morning at ten o'clock. But you must give me your parrot first, and the cough lozenges.'

'Here you are,' said Mr Wumble in delight. He handed the box to the dragon, and then placed the parrot on the dragon's shoulder. It didn't seem to mind a bit. It seemed to like the dragon much better than it had ever liked Mr Wumble. It nipped the dragon's ear very gently and spoke to him.

'Have you got your handkerchief, your hat, your umbrella, your cough lozenges and your scarf?' it said.

The dragon smiled with pleasure and said goodbye to Mr Wumble with glad tears in his eyes.

Mr Wumble walked briskly back to the palace, feeling very pleased with himself.

When he was taken to the princess he bowed very low and kissed her hand.

'Have you killed the dragon?' she asked in great excitement.

'No, but I have arranged that we shall have a fight tomorrow at ten o'clock,' answered Mr Wumble, banging his umbrella on the ground. 'I will conquer that fearsome dragon or die in the attempt.'

'Oh, you brave man!' said the princess. 'What do you ask in return for all this?'

'I ask that my wife, Mrs Wumble, may be fetched here to see the fight,' said Mr Wumble.

'But don't you want a palace or anything as well?' asked the princess in surprise. 'We usually give a palace, or a castle, and bags of gold to people who kill dragons.'

'Oh, well, I'd like a palace,' said Mr Wumble. 'And a few bags of gold would come in useful.'

'Very well,' said the princess. 'It shall be done.'

Mr Wumble was so excited that he hardly knew what to do. To think that he, ordinary Mr Wumble, was having an adventure with a princess, a dragon, bags of gold and a palace all mixed up together!

At half past nine the next morning Mr Wumble watched the aeroplane go off to fetch Mrs Wumble. At five minutes to ten it was back again. Mrs Wumble climbed out of the aeroplane and stared round at everybody.

'Where's Mr Wumble?' she said in a stern voice. 'He broke one of my best vases yesterday, and I want to ask him how he did it.'

'Oh, you can't ask him now,' said the princess. 'He's getting ready to fight a dragon. See, he's putting on his armour and trying his sword and shield.'

Mrs Wumble looked. She could hardly believe her eyes.

Mr Wumble was feeling tremendously excited. The gnome had brought him some shining armour to put on, and he was having a lovely time strutting up and down, waving his sword in the air, and shouting fiercely and loudly in a voice that Mrs Wumble had never heard him use before.

Just at that moment a roaring noise was heard from the hill, and everyone trembled. It was the dragon!

'Do not fear!' shouted Mr Wumble loudly.

Another tremendous roar came from the hillside, and a puff of smoke went up in the air.

'He is breathing out fire and smoke!' cried

everybody in terror.

'I will protect you all,' shouted Mr Wumble even louder.

'Oh, isn't he brave?' said the princess to Mrs Wumble.

Suddenly the dragon leapt into sight, gnashing his teeth so that they sounded like crashing rocks.

Mr Wumble felt a bit nervous. The dragon was looking very fierce, and Mr Wumble hoped the dragon wouldn't forget he was only pretending.

The dragon roared again and jumped up very high in the air. Mr Wumble thought the dragon was overdoing things.

I ought to have given him the cough lozenges afterwards, not before, he thought. *He may think that I would make a nice breakfast and forget all about my kindness yesterday. Well, if I'm going to be eaten, I might as well give the dragon a few jabs first.*

Mr Wumble dashed forward and lunged at the dragon with his sword. He leapt about, shouting and lunging all the time, keeping out of the way of the dragon's mouth as well as he could.

The dragon dodged about, and kept jumping high into the air, which was very annoying. Mr Wumble jabbed at the dragon once as it came down just beside him, and pricked him.

'Ow!' yelled the dragon. Then he turned round and put his mouth close to Mr Wumble's ear.

'If you do that again, I'll eat you!' he whispered fiercely. 'I thought we were only going to pretend to fight.'

'Sorry,' said Mr Wumble, glad that the dragon was pretending after all. 'Come on, let's dodge round each other again.'

Off they went again, while the watching people cheered and shouted, groaned and clapped as loudly as ever they could. Mr Wumble danced round and round the dragon, waving his sword merrily, and thoroughly enjoying himself. The dragon lashed about and roared fiercely, but neither of them hurt each other at all.

Then suddenly the dragon knocked Mr Wumble flat on the ground with his tail by mistake.

'If you do that again, I'll jab my sword into your tail, hard!' Mr Wumble said fiercely, getting to his feet.

'Very sorry,' said the dragon. 'Let's finish now, shall we? I feel as if I want to go and take another of those cough lozenges.'

'Come on then,' said Mr Wumble, and he shouted so loudly that the dragon jumped.

They pretended to go for each other more fiercely than ever, and at last the dragon rolled over with a dreadful groan, and lay stretched out on the ground.

'Go, fearful beast, before I kill you!' shouted Mr Wumble, loud enough for everyone to hear. 'Go back to your home far, far away, and never come to this land again.'

At once the dragon got up and galloped away at a great pace, groaning as it went. It went on and on and on, until it could be seen no more.

I hope my cough lozenges will really cure his cough, thought Mr Wumble to himself. He had fancied he heard it coughing as it ran away. Then he heard everybody cheering loudly, and Mrs Wumble flung her arms round his neck.

'Oh, my brave, brave Wumble!' she cried. 'I'm so proud of you. I won't say a word about that vase you broke!'

'I should think not!' said Mr Wumble in a stern voice. 'I hope you will never dare to grumble at me for a stupid thing like that, Mrs Wumble, when I have been busy killing a dragon!'

He went back to the princess, and she kissed him lightly on both cheeks, and they all went to the palace for a grand feast. Mr Wumble sat with Mrs Wumble and the princess at the head of the table, and was very happy. He kept his armour on, because he felt so smart in it, but it was very difficult to get his handkerchief out, so he had to take it off after a bit.

'And now about your palace?' said the princess.

'When would you like it?'

Mrs Wumble's eyes nearly fell out of her head.

'Oh, any time,' said Mr Wumble in a sort of don't-care voice.

'Oh, Mr Wumble, do let's have it now!' begged Mrs Wumble.

'Oh, very well, I'll have it now,' said Mr Wumble. 'And a few bags of gold, Your Highness, if it's all the same to you.'

The princess turned to her butler. 'See that everything's ready for Mr Wumble as soon as you can,' she said.

The butler bowed and went out.

After the meal was over, Mr and Mrs Wumble were taken to see their palace. It stood on the hill where the dragon had been, and was very grand indeed. Mr Wumble was delighted. He said goodbye to the princess, and then, taking Mrs Wumble's hand, he led her into the palace.

'Oh, you brave, brave man!' cried Mrs Wumble

again, and kissed him on his nose.

Mr Wumble smiled all over his face. He was the happiest man in the world, and there was only one thing he wished – he would very much have liked to have the dragon for a pet.

He was such a nice, sensible beast, thought Mr Wumble. *But, still, it would never have done. I only hope he's happy where he is, and has got rid of that nasty cough! As for the parrot, good riddance to bad rubbish, I say!*

Then Mr and Mrs Wumble settled down in their new palace, and you will be glad to know that, even though they were not a prince and princess, they lived happily ever after.

Cinderella

Cinderella

THERE WAS once a lovely little girl called Ella, who lived with her father, her stepmother and two stepsisters.

The stepsisters were ugly, for they were bad-tempered and unkind, and, as everyone knows, bad temper makes anyone ugly. Ella was very beautiful, and the sisters were jealous of her.

'She makes us look ugly!' they complained to their mother. 'Can't you send her away?'

But the stepmother couldn't do that, for Ella's father wouldn't let her. Instead she made her do all the kitchen work.

'If we make her dust and scrub, she will get scruffy and dirty,' she said, 'then no one will look at her.'

Poor Ella's clothes soon became so dirty and ragged that she was ashamed to be seen with her stepsisters in their beautiful clothes. She sat in the kitchen all alone, and wished she didn't have quite so much work to do.

One day her stepsisters found her sitting by the kitchen fire and laughed at her.

'Look! Look!' they cried. 'See the little cinder girl sitting among the cinders! We'll call her Cinderella!'

So they did, and soon everyone called her by that name and no other. She didn't complain, but simply did her work cheerfully and well, hoping that some day things would turn out better for her.

One morning the stepsisters were tremendously excited. They came dancing in to Cinderella, waving a big letter in their hands.

'What do you think?' they cried. 'The prince is giving a great dance and we're invited! He is going to choose a wife soon, and, who knows, he may choose one of us! Then we'll be very grand indeed!'

Cinderella listened, and wished she was going too. She helped her sisters all she could with their dresses, and ran about from morning to night for them.

When the great day came she did their hair elegantly, put some last stitches in their beautiful dresses, and buckled up their lovely shoes.

'Hurry! Hurry!' cried the sisters. 'Here comes the carriage to take us to the dance! Don't you wish you were going too, Cinderella – but you're *much* too ugly and dirty!'

They jumped in, waved goodbye and off they went. Cinderella watched them, and then went sadly to the kitchen, where she sat down and sighed.

'Now, my dear!' suddenly said a cheerful voice. 'What are you sighing about?'

Cinderella turned in surprise and saw an old woman standing near her, dressed in a peaked hat and red cloak.

'Who are you?' she asked in astonishment. 'And where did you come from?'

'I'm your fairy godmother,' laughed the old woman, 'and never you mind where I came from! Would you like to go to the prince's dance?'

'Oh, Godmother! I should simply *love* it!' cried Cinderella. 'But how can I? I've no dress, no carriage, no nothing!'

'Fiddlesticks!' said her godmother. 'You can have anything you want! Come outside with me and fetch a big pumpkin, and get me the rat trap and the mouse trap, and we'll see what we can do!'

Cinderella ran at once to fetch them, and soon brought back a fine yellow pumpkin, a trap with six rats in, and another trap with eight mice in. She put them down on the ground.

Her godmother waved her stick over the pumpkin and – lo and behold! – it changed into a wonderful golden coach, shining like a midday sun!

Then her godmother set free the six rats and waved

her stick over them. Hey presto! They changed into six of the finest black horses Cinderella had ever seen!

The eight mice were set free next, and changed into two splendid coachmen and six smart footmen. They harnessed the black horses in a moment and were soon ready in their places, the coachmen in front, five footmen standing stiffly behind, and one holding the door open politely for Cinderella.

'But, dear me!' gasped Cinderella, too astonished for anything, 'I can't possibly go to the prince's dance in this ragged old frock, Godmother! I would dirty that lovely coach!'

'Not at all!' laughed her godmother, and waved her stick over Cinderella.

What a marvellous, marvellous change! Cinderella's rags turned into a wonderful glittering dress, and on her head was a little circlet of gold. Little glass shoes twinkled on her small feet. Cinderella was too amazed to speak.

'Off you go!' said her godmother, pushing her into the carriage. 'Have a good time, Cinderella, but remember this – come home before the clock strikes twelve, for at midnight your dress will turn to rags and your coach, horses and men will turn back into pumpkin, rats and mice!'

Cinderella promised, and drove off with her head in a whirl. When she got to the dance everyone stared at her in surprise and wondered who she was, for never had they seen anyone so beautiful before. Her stepsisters didn't know her at all, but thought she must be some strange princess, come from a far-away land.

The prince couldn't believe his eyes when he saw her standing there, so shy and so lovely.

'If she is as good as she is beautiful,' he said, 'she is the wife for me!'

He hurried up to her, and asked her to dance with him, and was delighted to find that her nature was as sweet as her face. She wouldn't tell him her name nor where she came from, but he didn't mind *that* – he thought someone so lovely must surely be well known, and he would soon find out all about her.

Cinderella had never been so happy in all her life. She danced and ate, and then danced again. The prince was so good to her and looked so remarkably handsome that she lost her heart to him, and only wished she really *were* a princess so that she could marry him.

She forgot all about the time. Nine o'clock came, and ten o'clock. Eleven o'clock and – yes, it was striking midnight! In a flash Cinderella remembered what her godmother had said – her dress would turn to rags and her coach, horses and men to pumpkin, rats and mice.

She jumped up and left the prince's side. Down the palace steps she dashed to where her coach was waiting. As she went one of her glass shoes slipped off, and was left behind on the steps. The other she put into her pocket.

Alas! As she reached the bottom of the palace steps the clock finished striking twelve – and Cinderella's dress turned to rags, and her coach and horses vanished. She ran home barefoot through the dark streets, hoping she would be back before her sisters returned.

The prince dashed down the steps after her, and asked his footmen at the bottom if they had seen a lovely princess run out.

'No, Your Highness!' they answered in surprise. 'We have only seen a little ragged girl!'

The prince turned away sadly, and suddenly saw Cinderella's little glass slipper lying on the steps. He picked it up and put it in his pocket.

'Only my lovely little princess could have a foot tiny enough to fit this little shoe!' he said, smiling. 'So, tomorrow I will send round to every girl in the kingdom and make her try this slipper on! Whoever it fits shall be my wife!'

When the stepsisters got home they were full of

tales of the lovely, strange princess whom the prince had danced with so much.

'What was she like?' asked Cinderella, her heart beating very fast. 'Was she – was she at all like me?'

The stepsisters laughed loudly, and pointed their fingers mockingly at Cinderella.

'Like you!' they cried. 'Like a dirty little cinder girl! No, she wasn't in the least like you, Cinderella. She was very lovely, and had the sweetest face.'

Next day the prince's heralds came round with the little glass slipper, and proclaimed that whomsoever had a foot that would fit the slipper exactly should be the wife of the prince.

Dear me, the stepsisters *were* so excited! They each tried on the slipper, and squashed and squeezed their feet to try to get them inside. But it wasn't a bit of good, for they simply couldn't. Their feet were quite six sizes too large.

'Have you any other sister?' asked the herald.

'Only a dirty little cinder girl,' they answered. 'It's no good trying *her* foot. She didn't go to the dance.'

'The prince has ordered us to try every girl's foot,' answered the herald. 'Bring your sister here.'

Cinderella was fetched and – lo and behold – her little foot slid into the slipper and fitted it exactly!

'We have found her!' cried the heralds, and blew an enormously loud blast on their trumpets.

'You haven't, you haven't!' cried the sisters angrily.

'Fiddlesticks!' suddenly said a cheerful voice, and there was the fairy godmother again. She waved her stick over Cinderella, and once more she became dressed in her lovely dance clothes.

'Now do you know who she is?' asked the godmother, smiling.

The stepsisters didn't know where to look. To think that their ragged little hard-worked Cinderella should be this lovely glittering princess going to marry the prince!

Cinderella drove off to meet the prince, and

very soon the two were married in great state. They forgave the two stepsisters and asked them to the wedding, and the fairy godmother gave them some very good advice.

'Be good and kind,' she said, 'then you will lose those ugly faces and be sweet-looking instead!'

As for Cinderella, she and her prince lived happily ever after!

He Didn't Believe in Fairies

He Didn't Believe
in Fairies

THERE WAS once a farmer who didn't believe in fairies. You should have heard him laugh when fairies were mentioned! Why, he almost deafened you!

Now I expect you have heard it said that only those who believe in the little folk ever see them. Those who *don't* believe in them can't see them even when they are right under their noses! And often the fairies play tricks on these people just to each them.

Farmer Straw only believed in horses, cows, sheep and things like that. If you mentioned such things as dragons, unicorns, witches or pixies he would explode with laughter and call you a ninny. The fairy folk used to listen, and they laughed too. It really *was* funny to them, you see, to think that people said they weren't there, when *they* knew quite well they were!

Now Farmer Straw had a very fine mushroom field. So had his neighbour, Farmer Twinkle, and his other neighbour, Dame Busy. And in the autumn they all got up very early in the mornings and went mushrooming. When they sold their mushrooms in the market they made a great deal of money.

One night the little folk had had a dance in Dame Busy's field. It was a grand dance, with the grasshopper band playing rilloby-rill half the evening. That is the famous elfin tune, you know, that the grasshoppers know so well. There had been all kinds of games too, and a most delicious feast. And for once it hadn't ended at cock-crow, but just a little bit later.

Now this was a pity – because no sooner did the party break up than a rainstorm began! How it poured! How it pelted! The fairies, pixies and elves raced for the shelter of the mushrooms that had shot up in the night. They crouched beneath them and tried to keep their lovely frocks from being splashed. They hoped the rain would soon stop.

But it didn't. No, it went on and on and on. Goodness, the little folk couldn't possibly go home in it; they would be wet through! And see – there were lights in the farmhouses! People were getting up early to go mushrooming. Then what would happen to the fairies?

Dame Busy came out of her farmhouse with a big basket.

'Hey, little folk!' cried an elf. 'We shall be caught here if Dame Busy arrives before we go. She believes in fairies, you know, so she'll see us here under the mushrooms. Let us quickly run to the mushrooms in the other field – those belonging to Farmer Twinkle.'

So off the fairy folk scuttled through the wet grass and the rain, and soon they were safely sheltering under Farmer Twinkle's mushrooms. But, dear me, it wasn't long before the farmer opened *his* farmhouse door and came out to go mushrooming too!

So off went the fairies again – this time to Farmer Straw's mushrooms. And, bother me, if *his* door didn't open and out he came too to go mushrooming!

'Our luck is out this morning!' cried an elf. 'Whatever can we do? There are no more mushrooms to shelter us from this dreadful rainstorm! We shall have to go home and, oh, dear, what colds we shall get, for we shall be soaked through!'

'No, don't let's get wet!' cried a pixie. 'There's no need to! Let's each pick our mushroom and use it like the humans use umbrellas! We can carry them all the way home and never get wet at all! As for old Farmer Straw he won't see us for he doesn't believe in fairies! Ho, ho!'

'Ho, ho, ho, ho!' laughed all the little folk delightedly. Then they each picked a mushroom, and holding it above their bright little heads they made their way across the wet field down to the little wood where they lived.

Farmer Straw met them as he came to the field with his basket – yes, he met them – but he couldn't see the fairies, of course, because he didn't believe in them! All he saw was a row of big mushrooms walking solemnly along in the rain! He stood and stared with his mouth wide open. Then he gave a scream of fright and ran back to his farm.

'Oh! Oh! I'm going mad! I've seen mushrooms walking! Oh, what shall I do?'

'Don't be so silly!' shouted Dame Busy and Farmer Twinkle. 'It's only the little folk using them as umbrellas!'

'I don't believe in the fairies!' yelled Farmer Straw. 'No, that I don't.'

'Oh, well, if you like to believe in mushrooms walking off by themselves, instead of in the little folk, you do as you like,' said Dame Busy scornfully. 'But it seems to me to be much easier to believe in fairies than in walking mushrooms!'

Farmer Straw looked back at the row of bobbing mushrooms, half believing in the little folk for a moment – and just for that moment he saw a roguish face peeping at him from under a mushroom and caught the glint of a silvery pair of wings. But it was gone in a flash.

'Only ninnies believe in fairies,' he said. 'I'm not a ninny. There's something gone wrong with my eyes this morning, that's all – or else I'm not properly awake yet. Ho, I'd rather believe in walking mushrooms than a dozen fairies! That I would!'

But I wouldn't. Would you? Anyway, Farmer Straw lost all his mushrooms that day and you should have heard the little folk laugh about it! Farmer Straw thought it was the swallows twittering – but it wasn't.

The Sleeping Beauty

The Sleeping Beauty

ONCE UPON a time there lived a king and queen who had a dear little baby daughter born to them. They were very pleased indeed.

'When she is christened we will ask all the wise fairies to come for luck,' they said. So they sent out their invitations.

The christening day came, and all the wise fairies arrived. They were very pleased with the bonny little baby, and each bent over her in turn and waved her wand.

'I will give her a sweet face!' cried one.

'And I will give her a kind heart!' said another.

'And I will give her happiness!' cried a third.

Suddenly the christening hall grew dark, and a cold wind blew through it. In at the door came a bad-tempered fairy.

'Why didn't you ask *me* to the christening?' she stormed.

'I forgot. I'm so sorry,' said the king, though that wasn't really quite true. He hadn't asked the bad-tempered fairy because he didn't think she would do any good to the baby at all.

'Oh, you forgot, did you?' said the fairy. 'Well, *I* didn't forget. So I've come to see the baby – and I'll say this: when she's fifteen she shall prick her finger on the spindle of a spinning-wheel, and *die*!'

Then she swept out of the hall again, and left everyone staring at one another in fright.

'Oh, fairies!' cried the queen. 'Can't you break that wicked spell?'

'We can't break it,' said a fairy, 'but we can make it less cruel. When the princess grows to be fifteen she shall not die if she pricks her finger, but fall into a sleep for a hundred years, and everyone else in the palace with her!'

Well, that was quite bad enough. The king was very upset indeed, until he thought of a splendid plan.

'I shall have every spinning-wheel in the kingdom burnt,' he said, 'then the princess can't prick her finger on the spindle of one!'

So great bonfires were made all over the country, and everyone put spinning-wheels into the flames and burnt them to ashes. Then the king's mind was at rest.

All the gifts of the good fairies were seen in the princess as she grew up. She was healthy and happy, pretty and kind, and everyone loved her. She had never heard of the wicked spell cast on her by the bad fairy, so she didn't worry at all.

Now, when her fifteenth birthday came she had a great party and invited all her friends. After tea they began playing hide-and-seek up and down the palace.

The princess made up her mind to hide so cleverly

that no one would find her. So she ran right up to the very top of the palace and went into a tiny room in the roof. As she opened the door she saw an old woman sitting in a corner.

'Oh!' said the princess. 'I didn't know anyone was here!'

The old woman smiled at her. She was really the bad fairy, but the princess didn't know that. She was sitting spinning at a spinning-wheel.

'What is that wheel?' asked the princess. 'I've never seen one before.'

'Come and play with it,' said the old woman. The princess ran up, but alas! She pricked her finger on the spindle and immediately felt very sleepy.

'A-a-a-h!' she yawned. 'I'm *so* sleepy!'

Just at that minute the king and queen ran in to find the princess. The old woman vanished with a mocking laugh, and the princess showed them her pricked finger.

What a to-do there was! The king and queen

hurried her downstairs and put her safely to bed. But hardly had they done that than she fell fast asleep, and nothing would wake her.

Then one by one the king and queen, the courtiers and the servants, the dogs and the cats, fell asleep too, and soon nothing could be heard in the palace but the sound of snoring from the head cook, who had gone to sleep in a most uncomfortable position.

No sooner had everyone fallen asleep than a great thorn hedge grew quickly up all round the palace and completely hid it. No one could get through from the outside, and all the people in the kingdom were sad, for they knew that the bad fairy's spell had come true.

As the years went by brave princes tried to hack their way through the thorn hedge, but all to no use. They were pricked and torn so much that they went back defeated.

When a hundred years had gone by another prince made up his mind to try. He took a trusty sword and made his way to the great thorn hedge. Neither scratches nor cuts made him give up, and at last he had hacked a way right through to the palace.

Up the steps he went, staring in astonishment at all the sleeping servants. At last he came to where the pretty princess lay sleeping on her bed, with the king and queen beside her. She looked so very sweet that the prince bent down and gave her a soft kiss.

At once she awoke and smiled at him! The king and queen and everyone else stretched themselves, yawned and awoke too.

What rejoicing there was then! And how the bells pealed out when the news was told! All the people came running up to the palace to say how glad they were to have a king and queen once again.

And of course the prince married the princess, and they lived happily ever after.

The Lucky Fairy

The Lucky Fairy

HAVE YOU ever heard of the Lucky Fairy? If you haven't, I must tell you about her.

She lives in a tiny cottage just by the Lucky House, which is a queer sort of place. In the Lucky House grow hundreds of little lucky charms, which fairies wear round their necks to bring them good luck.

I have never been inside the Lucky House, but I know all about it, so I will tell you what you would see if you peeped inside the door.

You would see a perfectly round room with yellow shelves running all round it. On the shelves are put thousands of tiny pots, not much bigger than a thimble. The only window is in the roof, and through it the golden sun shines on to the little pots.

You would see a curious fire burning in the middle of the floor. There are no sticks, no coal to make it burn – there are just the flames springing up in four curling tongues. They are bright green in colour, and as they burn they send out a delicious scent, like nothing you can think of.

Sitting by the fire are four black cats, solemn and amber-eyed. At the beginning of every hour they take a grain of powder from a box by them and throw it into the fire, which immediately springs up twice as high as before. Then the cats get up and walk gravely round this strange fire seven times. They sit down again, and wait for the next hour to come.

On the seventh day of the seventh month the cats go to the little pots and look at them. Then they see that very tiny green charms have grown up in them and are ready for pulling. They are quite plain, oval in shape, and green in colour, and very, very tiny.

THE LUCKY FAIRY

These are the good-luck charms that every fairy may have once a year if they have been good. They are very precious indeed, and as it is considered a dreadful thing to be without one, you may be sure that it is very seldom that any fairy had to be refused one. There are exactly the right number grown and on the seventh day of the seventh month all the fairies come to get one.

They put them on a slender silver chain and wear them round their necks, and then they need not fear bad spells, and will have good luck for a whole year. Nobody knows exactly how they grow, for no one but the cats and the Lucky Fairy are allowed inside the Lucky House.

The Lucky Fairy is the one who gives out the little lucky charms. The fairies come to her cottage to get them, and show her a letter signed by the fairy queen to say they have been good, and then the Lucky Fairy gives them a new charm. She keeps one for herself too, of course.

Now for years and years the Lucky Fairy had managed her work beautifully. It was not difficult. All she had to do was fill four saucers with milk and take them to the black cats every day. She also had to water the little pots once a month. Then on the seventh day of the seventh month she had to go into the Lucky House and pull the little green charms from the pots and pop them into a basket ready to give them to the fairies.

It was very easy work, and she had plenty of time to go to dances, make herself pretty dresses of gossamer and petals, and talk to people who passed her way. She always had good luck, of course, because she wore her charm round her neck and didn't take it off day or night.

Then one day something happened.

A mouse went into the Lucky House. Nobody knows to this day how it got there. It smelt the delicious scent given off by the green flames, and it thought it would go and see what it was. *It might be a special kind of cheese, it might be fat bacon – it might even be both*, the mouse thought.

So it went to see. The room was dark except for the green flames, for it was night-time, and the sun had gone. The little mouse didn't see the four black cats sitting still by the fire! It thought they were bits of furniture, they kept so very still. It went close to the fire, sniffing – and then something happened!

The cats all saw the daring little mouse at the same moment, and with a shrill *meow* they pounced on him. In the crowd of claws he somehow escaped, and while the cats were clawing about, meowing loudly, he ran up on to the first shelf of pots. He crouched behind one, though it didn't really hide him, and waited there, his tiny heart beating far too loudly.

Soon the cats found he wasn't by the fire, and they began to sniff round the room. When they came to the shelf where he was, they became very much excited, and sniffed all the more. Suddenly their shining eyes saw him, and they pounced. Over went the pots, and rolled to the floor. Some of them broke to bits, and the little green charms that were growing in them were trampled to nothing.

The mouse leapt to another shelf, and the cats followed. More pots were broken, but the cats cared nothing for that. All they wanted was that mouse.

But they didn't get him. He found a tiny crack in the roof by the window, and squeezed himself through it, leaving them meowing below. Then they suddenly saw the broken pots, and knew that some of the lucky charms were spoilt. What a dreadful thing! Some of the fairies would have to go without them! What *would* they say!

The cats were very much upset. They cleared up the mess, and counted the broken pots. There were twelve that were broken.

'We must tell the Lucky Fairy in the morning,' said the biggest cat. 'How many did you count were broken, each of you?'

'I counted twelve,' said one cat.

'And I too,' said a second.

'And so did I,' said a third.

'I did too,' said the biggest cat. 'Four twelves are forty-eight. Oh, dear!'

Now the cats didn't stop to think that they had all counted the *same* twelve, so that really they only needed to have twelve more pots. They quite thought that they must have forty-eight, and they told the Lucky Fairy this when she brought them their milk the next morning.

'Oh, Lucky Fairy,' they said. 'In the night a small mouse came, and when we chased it forty-eight pots were broken. What is to be done about it? Forty-eight charms are destroyed.'

'What a dreadful thing!' cried the Lucky Fairy. 'It's never happened before. I must go to the queen and ask her what must be done.'

So she put on her new dress of red creeper leaves sewn with spider thread, and went to the queen's court. She told Her Majesty what had happened, and asked what was to be done.

'I must have some more pots made at once,' said the queen, 'and I must plant the lucky charm seeds in them myself. I have a few by me, which I have kept in case anything like this should happen. Forty-eight, did you say?'

'Yes, Your Majesty,' answered the fairy. 'The cats counted the broken pots themselves.'

Well, very fortunately the queen had enough seeds to spare, and with her own hands she planted them in forty-eight tiny pots that the court potter made that very day for her.

'It is a good thing that there are still many months to go before the lucky charms will be given out,' she said. 'These will grow fine, I think, and be ready when the others are.'

The pots were taken to the Lucky House, and the Lucky Fairy carefully placed them on the shelves. It was rather difficult to find room for them all, but she managed it. Then she gave the cats a good scolding, and told them that they were never to forget their duty again.

Time went by, and when the seventh day of the seventh month came round again, the cats told the Lucky Fairy that all the charms were ready to be given out.

'The forty-eight that the queen planted have grown just as well as the others,' they said. 'So there will be just enough as usual.'

All that day the fairies came crowding to the Lucky Fairy's cottage to get their new charms. They brought their letters with them to show that they had been good all the year round, and the Lucky Fairy was kept very busy handing out new charms from her full basket. She had pulled all the charms from the pots that morning, and had filled her basket to the very top.

When the evening came, her basket began to get empty. There were only about a hundred charms left. But the Lucky Fairy knew that some of the pixies might be late in coming to fetch theirs, for they had a good way to come. Sure enough, just as the sun was setting, she saw a little crowd of them come running through the wood towards her cottage.

'Sorry we're late,' they panted, 'but it's such a long way to come, and as the luck has just begun to wear out of our last year's charms, all sorts of silly things happened to prevent us coming quickly. Dinkie fell down and hurt his knee, and Pipkin lost his hat and had to go back for it. We shall be glad to have our *new* lucky charms again, and then perhaps we shall be more fortunate on our way back.'

The Lucky Fairy gave them all their new charms, and they hung them round their necks. Then they said goodbye and started back home. The Lucky Fairy looked down into her basket and found she had still got some charms left.

'Hie!' she called after the pixies. 'Are there any more of you to come?'

'No,' they called back. 'We're the last.'

The Lucky Fairy looked down into her basket in

astonishment. She counted the little green charms she had there, and found there were thirty-seven!

'Good gracious!' she said. 'What a curious thing! I've never had any left over before, except just my own new charm. If I take out my charm, I've still got thirty-six left. I wonder if everyone *has* been.'

She stayed up very late that night, and listened to see if anyone else came to fetch a charm. But nobody did. Everybody had got one. In the morning the Lucky Fairy counted the charms again that she had left over. She couldn't understand it. Then she suddenly gave a cry.

'Of course!' she said. 'The cats must have counted wrongly. Because they all four counted twelve broken pots they must have thought there were four times twelve – forty-eight! The silly old things! I must take these extra ones back to the queen.'

She took her own charm, and slung it round her neck. Then a very naughty thought came into her head.

Why not keep *all* the extra charms for herself, and wear them round her neck, under her frock? No one would ever know, for only she herself knew that there were any left over. What a lovely lot of good luck she would have if she did that!

The Lucky Fairy thought about this for such a long time that the four cats thought she had forgotten their milk. Soon she had made up her mind, and she quickly threaded all the thirty-six extra charms on her silver chain along with the charm she had already put there. Then she ran to fill the saucers with milk, and took them to the hungry cats.

It was not long before very good luck came to the Lucky Fairy. The next rainbow that came into the sky rested one of its ends just by her cottage. Of course, as you know, a crock of gold is always found at the rainbow's end, and when the Lucky Fairy saw it glittering so near she took her little spade and dug hard. Soon she came to a crock of gold, the biggest ever found at a rainbow's end, and this made her very rich!

Then, all in one week, six princes came riding by, and they each fell in love with her and begged her to marry them. She felt that perhaps a king might come, so she said 'No' to them all.

Not very long after that she found an old red ring, and when she rubbed it she found that she had got a wishing ring! Could anything be luckier! The Lucky Fairy could now get everything she wanted! She was very proud and pleased, and at once wished a castle for herself, and a hundred little servants to do her bidding. She dressed in most wonderful dresses, and everyone was astonished at her good luck.

It didn't stop there, and soon people began to wonder how it was that the Lucky Fairy had such marvellous things happening to her. Then one day one of the black cats caught sight of the silver chain that the fairy wore, and saw, with his sharp eyes, the many lucky charms on it. He thought about it for a day and a night, then he told the other three cats what he had seen.

'She has kept too many charms for herself,' he said. 'We must have counted wrongly that time we broke the pots.'

They talked about it for a long time, and then they found out their mistake. Only twelve pots had been broken, not forty-eight. The naughty Lucky Fairy must have kept thirty-six extra charms for herself.

'Tomorrow I will go to the queen and tell her,' said the biggest cat solemnly. So after the Lucky Fairy had given him his saucer of milk, he walked out of the Lucky House and made his way to the queen's court.

He told his story to her, and begged her pardon for having counted wrongly.

'But where are the extra lucky charms then?' asked the queen puzzled.

'The Lucky Fairy will know,' said the cat. 'She took all the charms from the pots as usual last time.'

At once the queen sent a message to the Lucky Fairy to go to her. She suddenly knew why the naughty little fairy had been so very, very lucky!

What a dreadful thing to do, to take all the lucky charms for herself! thought the queen. *I must scold her very severely.*

When the Lucky Fairy came to the palace the queen sternly told her to take her silver chain from her neck. The fairy began to tremble, for she guessed that the queen knew her secret. She took the chain from her neck and gave it to the queen.

'I thought so,' said the queen, taking it. 'You have kept far too many lucky charms for yourself! That was very dishonourable of you. I shall punish you.'

'Please forgive me,' begged the Lucky Fairy, beginning to cry. 'I know it was wrong, and I'll never do it again.'

'I shan't forgive you, unless you show me you are really sorry,' said the queen. 'What will you do to prove that you are?'

'Oh, I don't know!' wept the Lucky Fairy. 'I'll do anything! I'll give up all my lucky charms for a hundred years, if you like! But please let me still be the fairy who gives out the charms each year. I love my work, and I would hate not to do it. Please trust me still.'

'Very well,' said the queen, 'I will still trust you, but you must go without your own lucky charm every year, just to remind you of the naughty deed you have done. It won't hurt you to have a little bad luck for a change, after all the good fortune you have been having! You must give the spare to people who need them. And if ever there are any left over again, you must not keep them.'

'Yes, Your Majesty,' said the Lucky Fairy, drying her eyes. 'Whom would you like me to give them to?'

'You might take them to the world of boys and girls,' said the queen. 'There are lots of children who could do with a little good luck. You must find a good place to hide them in, so that only people who search for them may have them. Now go, and try to be good.'

The Lucky Fairy went away feeling very much ashamed of herself. She wondered wherever she could hide the little green charms. She wandered on and on until she came to our world, and she sat down in a green meadow.

And there at her feet she saw green clover growing, with its three tiny leaves spreading out to the sun.

'Why, the leaves of this plant are exactly like my little green charms!' cried the fairy in surprise. 'This would be a good place to hide them.'

So she carefully fastened one of the charms on to a clover leaf. When she had finished, you couldn't tell which was charm and which was clover.

'A four-leaved clover!' she cried. 'That shall be very lucky for whoever finds it!' Now I'll go and find another patch of clover and hide another charm there too.'

Off she went, and very soon she had fastened all her charms on to clover leaves, making four-leaved clovers. When she had finished she flew back to her cottage, for she no longer had her castle, and vowed she would never do a naughty thing again.

Whether she did or not, I don't know, but every year she hides whatever lucky charms are left over in patches of clover and makes the four-leaved clovers you sometimes find when you look hard enough.

And if you ever find one, do keep it, won't you, because it *may* bring you luck for a whole year. You won't know which of the leaves is the lucky charm from the Lucky House, but that doesn't matter – there's plenty of luck about it, if only you'll keep it!

Puss in Boots

Puss in Boots

ONCE UPON a time there was a miller who, when about to die, called his three sons to him.

'I have nothing much to leave you,' he said, 'but what I have is yours. You, eldest son, shall have my mill; you, second son, shall have my donkey. But, alas, third son, all I can leave you is my cat.'

The miller died and the eldest son took the mill. He allowed the second son to live there in return for the use of the donkey.

'But as for you,' he said to the youngest son, 'you must go and look after yourself. Your cat is no use to me.'

So the miller's youngest son sadly went out of his old home, with his cat following him.

He went to a shed and put all his belongings there. Then he looked at the cat and shook his head.

'Whatever can I do with you, Puss?' he said. 'You're no use to me, and I can't even feed you!'

'Cheer up, master,' said the cat. 'If you can find me a bag and a pair of boots, I'll soon show you that you've nothing to be sad about!'

The miller's son stared at the cat in great surprise.

Good gracious! he thought. *Never did I hear a cat speak before! This must be a truly wonderful creature who, perhaps, will be able to do wonderful things!*

He went straight away to get him a bag and a pair of boots.

Puss was very pleased with them. He proudly put on the big boots, and hung the bag over his back. Then he ran into the garden and plucked a fine fat lettuce, which he tucked into the bag.

The miller's son watched him in amazement. He

saw him stride across a field, and then lost sight of him.

Puss soon came to a rabbit hole. He lay down near it as if he were dead, leaving the mouth of his bag open, with the fine green lettuce peeping out.

Soon a rabbit came out of his hole. He smelt the lettuce and trotted over to it.

Only a dead cat near! he thought, and put his head into the bag for a good nibble at the lettuce leaves.

Quick as a flash, Puss pulled the string of the bag and the rabbit's head was caught. Puss pushed him right into the bag, slung it over his back, and marched off.

Very soon he arrived at the king's palace.

'I wish to see the king,' he said to the astonished guard.

He was taken to where the king sat on his throne. Puss bowed very low, and held out the bag to the king.

'Pray, Your Majesty, will you kindly accept this fine rabbit as a gift from my master, the Marquis of Carrabas?' he said.

The king was most surprised to see a cat who could speak.

'Go back to your master,' he said, taking the bag, 'and give him my thanks for his kind gift.'

Puss grinned and ran off.

Two days after, he caught two plump partridges, and put them into a bag. Off he went to the king, and stood bowing before the throne.

'Pray accept these plump birds as a gift from my master, the Marquis of Carrabas,' he said.

The king was delighted to see the marvellous speaking cat again, and accepted the gift. Then he told Puss to go to the kitchen and have a good meal, which the cat was most pleased to do.

Now before very long Puss heard that the king was going out driving with his beautiful daughter, and would pass by the riverside. An idea came into his head, and he ran off to his master, the miller's son.

'Master!' he cried. 'Will you trust me and obey me, if I ask you to do something strange? If you do it, maybe your fortune is made!'

'Tell me what it is,' said the miller's son.

'It is only this, master mine. Go to the river and swim in the place I show you. If anyone speaks to you, pretend you are the Marquis of Carrabas.'

The miller's son stared at the cat in astonishment, but because he knew Puss was very clever, he said he would do what he wanted him to do. Off he went with Puss to the river, undressed and began to swim.

Just as he was swimming, the king, his daughter and all the court were driving by. As they passed they heard a loud shout.

'Help! Help! Oh help! Help! My lord the Marquis of Carrabas is drowning!'

Everyone stopped at once, and looked around. Neither the king nor his court could see anyone but Puss in Boots, who beckoned to them anxiously.

'Go and see if you can help!' the king called to his nobles.

Off they all went and helped to drag the miller's

son out of the river.

Meanwhile Puss ran up to the king's carriage.

'Your Majesty, Your Majesty!' he cried. 'Whatever can my poor master do? A thief has stolen all his clothes, and he cannot pay his respects to you for he has nothing on but a bathing suit!'

'Dear, dear!' said the king, who by now was quite curious to see this Marquis of Carrabas. 'I will send one of my servants to the palace, and he shall bring back a suit of my own clothes.'

So a very smart suit was fetched, and the miller's son dressed himself. As he was tall and handsome he looked very fine indeed, and Puss was pleased with him.

The king was delighted to see the man whom he thought had sent him such fine rabbits and partridges, and he made him welcome.

'Come in for a drive, marquis,' he said, and the miller's son got into the carriage.

Puss went on ahead of the carriage with another

plan in his head. Soon he came to a field where mowers were cutting grass.

'Hie!' he called to them in a fierce voice. 'When the king comes by and asks you whose these fields are, say they belong to the Marquis of Carrabas! If you don't, I'll have your heads cut off!'

The mowers shook in their shoes to hear a cat talking. When the king came up and asked whose fields they were cutting they answered what the cat had told them.

'They are the fields of the Marquis of Carrabas, Your Majesty!'

The king looked at the miller's son and said, 'What fine fields you have, marquis!'

While this was happening, Puss ran to a cornfield in which were men reaping corn.

'Hie!' he called fiercely. 'When the king comes by and asks you whose these fields are, say they belong to the Marquis of Carrabas! If you don't, I'll have you made into mincemeat!'

The poor reapers shivered and shook. The king soon came by and asked whose cornfields they were cutting.

'They are the cornfields of the Marquis of Carrabas, Your Majesty!' they answered.

'What fine cornfields you have,' said the king, turning to the miller's son, and thinking what a rich man he must be. *In fact*, thought the king, *he would make a fine husband for my daughter.*

Now all these fields really belonged to a wicked wizard who lived in a castle not very far off. Puss ran to it and knocked at the door. The wizard opened it.

'Good day, sire,' said Puss, bowing very low. 'On my travels I have heard how wonderful you are, so I have come to see you.'

'Then pray come in,' said the wizard, very pleased indeed.

Puss went in, and they began to talk.

'Is it true,' said Puss, 'that you can change yourself into any animal you wish?'

'Quite true!' said the wizard, and changed himself suddenly into an enormous lion to show Puss how clever he was.

The cat was so frightened and astonished that he ran up the window curtains to the very top, and stayed there until the wizard changed back to his own shape again. Then Puss jumped down.

'Sire!' he cried. 'You are wonderful. Can you be clever enough to change yourself into a *little* animal? That must be even more difficult than turning into a big one!'

'Not at all!' said the wizard, delighted to show off his cleverness. 'Look here!'

In a second he changed himself into a tiny brown mouse, and ran over the floor to Puss.

Aha! That was exactly what that clever cat wanted. He pounced on the mouse and gobbled him up!

'Not much of a meal,' said Puss, licking his lips. 'But that makes an end to the wicked wizard anyhow. Now this castle can belong to my dear master!'

Just at that moment, up drove the king and his court, and the cat ran out to the gate to lead them to the castle.

'Welcome! Welcome!' he cried. 'Three times welcome to the castle of the great Marquis of Carrabas!'

The king gazed at the splendid castle and then turned to the miller's son in surprise.

'What a fine castle!' he said. 'I have not such a grand one in the whole of my kingdom!'

The miller's son said nothing. Indeed, he was so surprised at everything that he really didn't know what to say.

When the company entered the castle they found a feast waiting for them. The wicked wizard had really prepared it for his friends, but they, seeing the king arrive, did not dare enter.

The king feasted well, and felt more and more pleased with the miller's son. At last he turned to him and said, 'Marquis, I like you more and more. I have never met a man whom I would like so much as you for my daughter's husband. Let me make you a prince, and then if you will, you may marry the lovely princess!'

Now the prince and princess had had plenty to say to each other in the carriage, and they had fallen in love at once, so they were delighted to hear the king's speech.

'But, dear love,' whispered the miller's son to the princess, 'I am really only a miller's son, and I owe all this to my clever cat, Puss in Boots.'

'What does that matter to me?' smiled the princess. 'It is enough that I love you.'

So with great rejoicing and feasting the miller's son and the princess were married, and went to live in the castle that used to belong to the wicked wizard.

As for Puss in Boots he waited on them both faithfully, and was as proud as could be of the lovely bride he had won for his master.

Oriell's Mistake

Oriell's Mistake

ONCE UPON a time the fairy queen sent two little fairies out into the world.

'Now see what good and noble things you can do,' said the fairy queen as she said goodbye to them, 'and in a year come back to me and tell me what you have learnt and what great things you have done.'

'Very good, Your Majesty,' answered the fairies, bowing low.

'I shall want one of you to become the Lord High Chamberlain of Fairyland,' said the queen, 'so do the best you can to prepare for such a high position.'

Off went the two fairies, feeling very excited and pleased.

'Let's find somewhere to live first,' said Oriell, who was a fine, tall fairy with magnificent wings.

'Yes, let's,' answered Coran, a smaller fairy, not dressed nearly so grandly as Oriell.

So for that day they flew about seeking for a home. When they met again at night Oriell asked Coran where he was going to live.

'I'm going to live in Rosemary Cottage, just under the eaves,' answered Coran. 'There's a nice peasant woman there and a dear little girl.'

'Pooh! Fancy choosing a cottage to live in when you may, perhaps, be going to be the Lord High Chamberlain of Fairyland!' exclaimed Oriell. 'Now I've found a glorious place!'

'Where?' asked Coran.

'On the top of the church steeple!' said Oriell proudly. 'I asked the weathercock if he minded, and he said he'd be very glad to have me. He's a grand fellow, that old weathercock – he can tell no end of stories about people. I shall learn a lot of things from him, I can tell you!'

'It sounds a very nice place,' said Coran, 'and I hope you'll like it.'

'Oh, I am *sure* to like it,' answered Oriell. 'Besides, there's the West Wind to talk to. The weathercock says he's always about, and can tell all sorts of thrilling stories.'

'But you'll come down and see me sometimes, won't you?' asked Coran, feeling rather left out.

'Oh, yes, I expect so,' said Oriell grandly. 'Now, goodbye, I'm off to my steeple!' And away he flew.

Coran flew to Rosemary Cottage and cuddled down under the eaves. He soon fell asleep and didn't wake until he heard a lark singing next day.

Then began a very busy time for Coran. He used to listen to the peasant woman and the little girl talking together.

'Old Mother Brown is ill,' the woman said. 'You

must take her some broth, my dear.'

The little girl went off, carrying the broth carefully, and Coran flew just behind her. When he saw the delight of poor old Mother Brown's face as she tasted the steaming broth he felt quite funny inside.

'I *must* do something to make people look glad like that,' Coran decided, 'even if it's only a little thing.'

He soon found that if he listened to what the peasant woman talked about every day he would have lots of things to do.

'Poor little Johnnie has broken his leg,' said she. 'I wish we could help him.'

Coran flew off at once and sat on the end of Johnnie's bed and told him fairy stories for a week!

'Cobbler Jones has got his wife ill and no money to pay for the doctor!' sighed the peasant woman the next day, looking to see if *she* had any money to spare for him.

Coran found Cobbler Jones's house and slipped

three gold pieces under his pillow, and was most delighted to see the cobbler's look of amazement and joy the next morning!

Week after week Coran joined in the village life, and, unseen and unheard, did his best to bring a joyful look to the faces of the people around him.

Oriell, from the top of the steeple, sometimes used to see him slipping in and out of the cottages.

'Silly little Coran!' he said. 'How can he expect to learn anything down there?'

'Creak – creak! You are a clever fellow, Oriell,' said the weathercock. 'You have chosen well to live up here where you can see all that is going on down below.'

'Tell me the story of the king who lived in that castle garden,' begged Oriell.

And the weathercock obligingly told him. Then up came the West Wind and began to tell marvellous tales of all the countries he had been to.

'Oh, what a fine life you have!' sighed Oriell. 'But

never mind, when I'm Lord High Chamberlain of Fairyland *I'll* have great adventures too!'

At last the year came to an end and both fairies returned to Fairyland.

'What have you learnt, and what have you done?' asked the queen.

'I've only learnt one thing,' said Coran, a little ashamed. 'I've learnt how to bring a glad look into people's faces – but I've done no noble things. I've been so busy learning just that one thing, you see.'

'And what have you learnt, Oriell?' asked the queen.

'Oh, I've learnt a lot,' said Oriell proudly. 'I've learnt all about different countries, and I've learnt how to behave if I should meet kings and princes, for the weathercock has told me. And I've done a very noble thing: I've lived on a church steeple, high above everyone else, and watched their daily lives.'

The queen turned to Coran and held out her hands.

'*You* shall be Lord High Chamberlain,' she said gently. 'Oriell has done a little thing and called it great. He must go and learn for another year. You have done a great thing and thought it little. You will make a splendid Lord Chamberlain.'

And she was quite right. He did!

The Story of Rumpelstiltskin

The Story of Rumpelstiltskin

ONCE UPON a time there lived a miller and his wife. They had one daughter, who was so clever and so beautiful that her father and mother were always boasting about her.

They not only boasted about things she *could* do, but about things she couldn't do, and one day when the miller went to see the king he began telling him of all the marvellous things his daughter had done.

'Your Majesty!' he said. 'You can have no idea how clever my daughter is! Last year she spun straw into silver – yes, silver! – and this year she is going to spin it into gold!'

'What!' cried the king in astonishment. 'Spin straw into gold! Impossible!'

Like all boasters, the miller could not bear to have his story disbelieved.

'I assure you, Your Majesty,' he said, 'my words are true. My clever and beautiful daughter is going to spin all my straw into gold for me, and I shall be a rich man.'

The king listened and wondered.

'Miller,' he said, 'such a marvel I have never seen in my life. You must send your daughter to my palace, and tell her I want to see her do this thing of which you tell me. I have plenty of straw that I should dearly like to see spun into gold.'

The miller began to feel frightened. He knew quite well that, clever as his daughter was, she could certainly *not* spin straw into gold! He began to make excuses, and to say that his daughter could not come.

'I'll cut off your head if you don't send her tomorrow!' said the king, who was quite determined that, if there was any gold about, he was going to get a good share of it.

The miller groaned loudly, bowed and left the palace. He ran home and told his wife all about it.

'You foolish man!' she scolded. 'Now we shall lose our heads because of your silly tale!'

'You are as bad as I am,' he grumbled. 'I heard you tell the neighbours that our girl was clever enough to spin straw into gold, and I told the king. What are we to do?'

'We must send our daughter to the palace,' said the miller's wife, 'and hope that because of her beauty the king will forgive her for not being able to do as you say.'

So the next day the miller's daughter was hurried to the palace. She was most astonished, for neither her father nor her mother told her why.

They left her with the king, who took her by the hand to a large bare room filled with straw.

'And now, my pretty one,' he said, 'you must spin

all this straw into gold for me. Tomorrow morning I shall come back to you, and if you have not done as I command, I shall have your lovely head cut off.'

With that he went out of the room, and locked the door. The young girl sat there in the greatest astonishment.

'Spin straw into gold!' she said to herself. 'Why, whoever heard of such a thing! No one can do that! Whatever does the king mean?'

She sat and thought for some time, and then she began to weep bitterly.

'I don't want to have my head cut off,' she sobbed. 'It isn't fair to expect me to do an impossible thing!'

She wept all morning, and made her pretty eyes red. Just as she was wondering if anyone was going to bring her any dinner, she heard a noise at the window.

She looked up. In hopped the funniest little creature with a long black tail that kept twirling in and out, and round and round.

'Now, now!' said the creature. 'What's all this

crying about? Tell me what is the matter, and maybe I can help.'

'Oh, sir!' wept the young girl. 'The king has shut me up here and told me to spin all this straw into gold. If I haven't finished it by tomorrow morning, I shall have my head cut off.'

'Dear, dear, dear!' said the little creature, twirling his tail in and out. 'What a to-do, to be sure! Now what will you give me if I do your task for you, and spin all this straw into gold?'

'Oh, I will give you this lovely necklace of mine,' said the young girl.

The little creature sat down at the spinning-wheel and began to spin. The young girl watched him in amazement, for as the straw went whirring through his fingers it changed into shining threads of gold!

Soon great piles of gold lay where the straw had been, and before night came every piece had been changed into pure gold.

At last the little man jumped up, took the girl's

necklace and said goodbye. He twirled his black tail three times and then jumped straight out of the window.

The young girl went to sleep with an easy mind, and was awakened by the king coming into the room to see what she had done the day before.

When he saw all the straw gone, and gold heaped up all around, he was too much astonished to speak. He stood there with his mouth open and stared.

This is good – very good! he thought. *I will have more of this!*

So after he had given the miller's daughter a good breakfast he took her into a yet bigger room, where there was twice as much straw as before.

'Now, my pretty one, turn all this into gold for me,' he said. 'If not, I'll have your head cut off!'

The young girl could hardly believe her ears. Turn all this straw into gold too! Oh, dear, oh, dear! What bad luck had come to her! She sat down at the spinning-wheel, weeping bitterly, and tried to do as the little creature had done yesterday. But the straw remained straw, and no gold came at all.

Suddenly, in at the window, hopped the tiny creature again, twirling his tail even more quickly than before.

'Stop crying!' he said. 'I'll do it all for you if you'll give me your diamond ring.'

The girl dried her eyes at once, and joyfully watched the little man spinning the straw into gold.

Whirr-whirr-whirr! went the wheel, and soon piles of golden threads lay on the floor. But the young girl could not see for the life of her how it was done.

When night came the creature took her diamond ring, called goodbye and jumped out of the window with a last twirl of his tail.

The king was delighted next morning to see the room filled with shining gold.

'You are certainly a wonderfully clever little maiden,' he told the miller's daughter. 'Now come with me to a yet bigger room. If you can spin all the straw there into gold, I will marry you and make you my queen.'

He took the girl to a huge room filled with piles of straw, and there he left her. He was most pleased with all the gold he had, and thought that search how he might, he would surely never be able to find a cleverer or lovelier girl than the miller's daughter. It would be so very useful to have a wife who could spin him gold whenever he wanted it!

No sooner had the king gone than the little creature hopped in at the window again, twirling his tail round and round.

'What can you give me this time, if I spin the straw into gold?' he asked.

'I haven't anything more at all I can give you,' said the maiden sadly.

'I shan't do it for nothing,' said the little man. 'I know – you must make me a promise!'

'What shall I promise?' asked the maiden.

'Promise me,' said the creature, 'that when you are

queen and have a little baby born to you, you will give it to me.'

The miller's daughter promised, for she didn't think for one moment that the king meant to marry her, so she thought she would be quite safe.

The little creature set to work and soon finished spinning all the straw. Then he said goodbye and went, and the last thing the girl saw of him was a twirl of his tail.

Now the king was so delighted with his third lot of gold that he kept his word, and, much to her delight, married the miller's daughter.

She made a good queen, and was overjoyed when a little baby boy was born to her. She was hugging him close one day, when who should hop into the room but the little creature again.

'What have you come for?' asked the queen in fright.

'Have you forgotten your promise?' asked the little man, twirling his tail. 'I want your baby!'

'Oh! oh!' cried the queen, suddenly remembering the promise she had made. 'No, little creature, no! I cannot give you my darling baby. Ask me anything else but that!'

The little man grinned and twirled his tail even more quickly.

'I'll give you a chance,' he said. 'Find out in three days what my name is, and you shall keep your baby!'

Then off he hopped.

The queen thought of all the names she knew, and when next the little creature came, she told him them.

'Is it Arthur, or John or Peter? Paul or William or James?' she asked.

But no matter what name she said the creature laughed and shook his head.

Next day the queen sent messengers all over her kingdom to collect the strangest names there were. *For surely*, she thought, *such a peculiar creature must have a peculiar name!*

'Is your name Spindle-Legs, Squinty or

Roll-Around?' she asked. 'Is it Twisty-Tail, Bandyshanks or Crooked-Nose?'

'No, no, no!' shouted the little creature, twirling his tail fast. 'Tomorrow I will have your baby!'

The poor queen sent messengers out once more, but, alas, they could find no more strange names. One, however, had a strange story to tell.

'I was in a dark forest,' he said, 'when I suddenly heard a noise of singing. I crept up to see who it was, and in a little clearing among the trees I saw a tiny red-roofed cottage. In front of it danced the oddest little creature with a long black tail that twirled in and out, and round and round. On his head was a tray of new-baked loaves, and they all bounced up and down as he danced. The song he sang was this:

'Today I brew, tonight I bake,
Tomorrow the queen's child I shall take;
For guess as she will, she never will know
That my name is RUMPELSTILTSKIN, oh!'

The queen listened eagerly, for she knew quite well who the little black-tailed creature was. When the next day came she saw that he had brought a basket to take away her baby.

'Well, do you know my name?' he asked.

'Is it Hugh?' she asked, pretending not to know.

'No, it is not!' shouted the little creature, twirling his tail.

'Is it Joseph then?'

'No, it is not!' shouted the tiny man, twirling his tail so fast that it really couldn't be seen.

'Is it Charles?' asked the queen, sadly as if she could think of no more names.

'No it is *not*!' shouted the creature, and jumped to get the baby. But the queen held him off.

'Then it must be RUMPELSTILTSKIN!' she cried.

'Oh, oh, oh!' screamed the little man in a rage. 'The witches have told you – yes, they have!'

He stamped on the ground, and twirled his tail so

hard that it came right off and lay on the floor. He picked it up, popped it into the basket, and jumped clean out of the window.

And that was the last that the queen ever heard of him, though it is said that he still goes round trying to find someone to sew his tail on again for him!

The Land of
Golden Things

The Land of
Golden Things

ONCE UPON a time there was a king who was very poor. He hadn't even a palace to live in, and that made him very sad. He had a crown to wear, it is true, but it wasn't made of real gold, and it only had eight precious stones in it.

He lived alone in a cottage with his little daughter, Rosamunda. He had spent all his money in going to war with another country, and had lost the battle. His people were too poor to help him – so there he was, a king no better than a pauper.

His cottage was built in a lovely place looking out over the blue sea. He had one cow that gave him creamy white milk, four hens that laid him eggs every day, and an old servant woman who cooked nice, simple meals for him, grew fine vegetables in the little garden and looked after Rosamunda.

The king was very unhappy. He longed for a palace, he longed for a treasure chest filled with gold, he longed for hundreds of servants, fine clothes and beautiful furniture. His little daughter grieved to see him so miserable, and tried to make him laugh and smile – but it was very difficult. Rosamunda was happy. She knew she was a princess, but she was glad she didn't live in a palace. She liked to feed the four hens and milk the gentle cow. She loved to paddle in the warm pools and walk out on the windy hills.

Best of all she liked to work in the little garden that belonged to the cottage. She loved to grow bright flowers and pick them for the jugs and bowls indoors. She used to take big bunches of sweet-smelling roses to her father, and make him look at how lovely they were.

'Look, Daddy,' she would say. 'Smell them. Aren't they beautiful?'

But the king wouldn't bother about them. If they had been made of silver or gold he would have seized them eagerly – but they weren't.

One day in the summertime he had a birthday. Rosamunda planned to give him a lovely present. She had a little rose tree in a pot, one that she had grown all by herself, and she meant to give her father this.

She gave him a birthday hug, and then suddenly brought out the dear little tree. It was covered with tiny pink buds and blossoms, and was just like a fairy-tale tree. Rosamunda felt sure her father would love it.

But, do you know, he didn't even look at it properly! He just glanced at it, and said 'Thank you, my dear,' and nothing else at all. He didn't say, 'Oh, what a lovely little tree! How I shall love to have it and look after it!' Rosamunda was dreadfully disappointed.

'Daddy, darling, you must be sure to water it every

single morning before the sun gets hot,' she said to him. 'It is rather a delicate little tree, so please see that it gets enough to drink.'

The king put it on the windowsill in his tiny bedroom, and then forgot all about it. He sat down and thought of the birthday he would have had if he had been a king with lots of money and a rich kingdom.

I should have had a hundred guns fired off, he thought. *Then people would have come to my throne bringing gorgeous presents. At night I would have given a grand party, and had kings and queens, princes and nobles for my guests. Wouldn't it have been fine?*

He made himself so miserable, grieving over this, that for quite a week he forgot to smile at Rosamunda. She was sad because she loved him. She felt sure too that he had forgotten to water the little tree she had given him.

One bright morning the king went for a walk through the fields that lay behind his cottage. As he went on his way a stranger approached him.

He was a fine-looking youth, tall and strong.

'Can I help you?' asked the king, seeing that the stranger seemed to have lost his way.

'That would be kind of you,' said the youth. 'I want to get back to the place where I have left my carriage, and I cannot find the way. It was by a lovely little blue stream that ran through a wood.'

'You have wandered for miles then,' said the king. 'I know the stream. Let me take you back myself. I am sorry I have no servant to guide you, but there is only the old woman in the cottage. I am a king, but have none of the things a king should have, as you can see – except for my crown.'

'That is very good of you,' said the stranger. So he and the king walked over the fields together, and after about two hours came to where the carriage had been left.

How the king stared when he saw it! It was made of pure gold, and shone in the sun so brightly that the king was dazzled when he looked at it.

There was a coachman there, clad in a golden livery, and eight footmen, all in gold breeches and coats of fine brocade.

'How rich you must be!' the king said enviously.

'Let me drive you to my kingdom, and you shall see it,' said the strange youth. 'It is supposed to be one of the most wonderful places in the world.'

The king stepped into the carriage. The coachman flicked his golden whip, and the horses started forward. How fast they went! The king knew they must have some sort of magic in their blood for they went too fast for him to see anything out of the windows at all. Trees, houses and hedges flashed by in a long line.

At last the carriage stopped in front of a vast golden palace. The king shut his eyes after giving it one glance for it was so dazzling. He went up the golden steps, feeling quite dazed.

The stranger gave him a wonderful meal served on golden plates with an edging of diamonds. He drank from a golden goblet studded with red rubies and green emeralds. Servants clad in rich golden draperies stood in dozens around the golden hall. How the king envied all this richness!

'If only I had a little of your marvellous store of gold,' he said to the stranger, 'how happy I should be!'

'You shall have as much as my carriage will hold when it takes you home again,' said the youth. 'I have so much that I am glad to get rid of some of it.'

After the meal the king went to see the treasure house. There were not only bags of gold there, and chests filled to the brim with golden bars, but also rare treasures. There was a golden apple that could make anyone who was ill feel better at once merely by holding it in his hand. There was a goblet set with sapphires that was always full of the rarest wine in the world, no matter how much was drunk from it.

The king looked at all these things longingly. Then he saw a beautiful mirror, and he picked it up to look at it.

'That mirror will show you the picture of anyone you think of,' said the stranger. 'Think of someone now, and take a look in the mirror.'

The king at once thought of one of his generals, and looked into the mirror. A picture came there, and he saw an old bent man working in a potato field. When the man stood up, the king saw that it was his old general.

'Dear, dear!' he said sadly. 'To think that my famous old general should be working in a potato field!'

Then he thought of the king who had defeated him, and immediately a new picture came into the mirror. It showed a fat, ugly man sitting at a well-laden table. He wore a heavy crown, and he frowned at his queen, who was sitting beside him. She was speaking sharply to him, and though the king could not hear what was being said, he knew that she was cross with his old enemy and was scolding him.

'Aha!' he said. 'So my foe has grown fat, and his

queen leads a miserable life!'

Then he turned to the youth. 'This is a marvellous mirror,' he said. 'May I have it, for it would pass away many a weary hour for me?'

'What will you give me for it?' asked the youth. 'It is a very valuable thing.'

'I have so little that I can give,' said the king. 'Would you like a cow? Or a hen perhaps?'

The youth laughed. 'No,' he said. 'You shall give me whatever you see first tomorrow morning! As soon as you set eyes on it, it will vanish away to my kingdom. It will be amusing to see what comes!'

The king took away the mirror happily. He saw many bags of gold stowed away in the carriage that was to take him back to his cottage, and on the way home he made all kinds of plans.

'I shall build myself a fine house,' he decided, 'and get a new crown. Rosamunda shall have her first silken dress and a golden necklace.'

It was late when he arrived back at the cottage. The

footman helped to dump all the bags of gold under the tree in the little garden, and then off went the golden carriage into the night.

The king was tired. He undressed and got into bed, thinking of the wonderful mirror.

I shall look at the little rose tree that Rosamunda gave me for my birthday, he thought. *That shall be the very first thing I set eyes on. It is about the only nice thing in this bedroom. I am sure the stranger will be pleased to see it arriving in his kingdom.*

He fell asleep. When the early-morning sun streamed into his room, he still slept. But Rosamunda was awake. She was out in the garden singing merrily. She looked up at her father's bedroom, and wondered if he was awake. She caught sight of the little rose tree on his windowsill, and she saw that it was drooping.

'Poor little tree,' it wants water,' she said. 'I will creep into Daddy's room and water it before the sun gets hot.'

She took a jug, filled it with water and went up to

her father's room. She knocked, and then knocked again. When she got no answer, she opened the door and peeped in. She saw the king lying fast asleep in bed, so she ran lightly across the floor to the window, and began to water the rose tree.

At that moment the king awoke. He remembered that he meant to look at the tree first of all, so he opened his eyes and glanced across at the window where the tree stood.

But Rosamunda stood there in front of it, watering it! The king saw her immediately – and then she vanished before his eyes!

'Oh!' said the king in horror. He sat up and rubbed his eyes. Then he looked again. There stood the little tree, and there on the floor lay the jug that his little daughter had been using. But Rosamunda was quite gone.

'She's vanished to the Land of Golden Things!' groaned the king. 'Oh, what shall I do?'

He got up and went to the window. Then he saw all

the bags of gold lying under the tree in the garden, and in delight he rubbed his hands and laughed. He forgot all about Rosamunda, and dressed quickly in order to go and run his hands through the golden coins.

He thought no more of his little girl all that day till the old servant came to him in distress and said that she could not find Rosamunda anywhere.

Then the king remembered what had happened, and told the servant about it.

'Oh, oh, oh!' she sobbed, wringing her hands. 'To think of my little pet all alone in a strange land! Oh, you wicked man, to forget all about your little lamb like this! What is gold compared with Rosamunda's silken hair, merry eyes and loving smile?'

The king suddenly felt miserable. How could he have forgotten his happy little daughter? He went red with shame, and turned away his head. But how could he get Rosamunda back? He did not know the way to the Land of Golden Things.

All that week the king missed his little daughter badly. He could remember Rosamunda's sweet smile and her loving voice. He could remember the feel of her warm hugs and kisses. He longed to hear the patter of her little feet. But instead of Rosamunda in the garden, he had bags and bags of gold.

Then he remembered the wonderful mirror he had brought back with him, and he looked into it. He thought of Rosamunda, and immediately the mirror showed him a picture of her.

She was standing in a garden, picking roses from a glittering bush. But alas for Rosamunda! The roses were golden, and had no smell, no softness, no beauty.

The king watched his little daughter in the mirror. He saw big tears streaming down her cheek as she held the hard rose in her hand. He knew how much she must miss her own little cottage garden, with its pretty, sweet-smelling flowers growing everywhere from seeds she herself had planted.

'Oh, if only I could get my little daughter back

again, I would be happy here for the rest of my days!'
he said. 'I would willingly give back this gold and this
marvellous mirror if I could have Rosamunda in their
place! I have been a foolish man, always pining for
riches when beside me I had Rosamunda, worth more
than a hundred thousand bags of gold. How hard she
tried to please me, how sweet she was, and how
she loved me!'

The unhappy king walked out into the fields and
wept loudly. Suddenly he saw the bright stranger
again and he ran up to him eagerly.

'Tell me about Rosamunda!' he cried. 'Is she
wanting me? Is she sad?'

'Very sad,' said the stranger gravely. 'Will you
take her back, in exchange for the gold and the mirror,
O King?'

'Willingly, willingly!' cried the king with joy.
'I am cured of my foolishness. I no longer wish for
anything more than my little daughter. If I have her,
I am richer than any king in the whole world!'

'She is in my carriage over there,' said the stranger with a smile.

The king turned and saw the golden carriage standing in a narrow lane nearby. He scrambled through the hedge, tearing his clothes terribly, but he did not care one bit! There was Rosamunda looking out of the carriage. When she saw her father she gave a shriek of delight, opened the door and fell into his arms. How they hugged and kissed one another! How they laughed and cried! They quite forgot about the stranger.

By the time they remembered him he was gone. Vanished too were the bags of gold, the mirror and the wonderful golden carriage. But the king laughed to see them gone. He had Rosamunda back, and that was all he cared about.

'Daddy, you seem different,' said Rosamunda. 'I believe you love me after all. We will be happy together now, won't we?'

'We will!' said the king. 'You and I will work in the

garden together, and go for walks together, and row on the sea together. Won't we be happy, Rosamunda?'

'Throw your crown away, Daddy!' cried the little girl. 'Don't be a silly old king with no money and lots of frowns and sighs. Be a nice daddy, and smile and laugh every day!'

She took the crown from the king's head and threw it into a nettle bed! The king looked horrified at first – but soon he laughed. And never again did he want to be rich, for he knew that was foolishness. Now he and Rosamunda are as happy as the day is long.

As for the little rose tree she gave him for his birthday, they planted it out in the garden. It has climbed all over the cottage now, and if you happen to visit them in the summertime, you will see how lovely it is.

The Hardy Tin Soldier

The Hardy Tin Soldier

THERE WERE once twenty-five tin soldiers. They shouldered their guns and looked straight in front of them; their uniform was red and blue, and very splendid.

The first words they heard in the world were 'Tin soldiers!' when the little boy who had been given them for his birthday took off the lid of their box and saw them.

He put them all out on the table. Each soldier was exactly like the rest, except the last one of all, and for some reason or other he had only one leg. But he stood as firmly on it as all the others did on two.

Nearby the soldiers stood a castle made of cardboard. In front of it was a little lake made of a piece of glass on which little wax ducks swam. It was all very pretty – but the prettiest of all was a little lady, who stood at the open door of the castle. She was a tiny doll, and was dressed in white, with a piece of blue ribbon over her shoulders for a scarf. She wore a pink rose, and looked the daintiest little creature. She was a dancer and stretched out both her arms. One of her legs too was lifted so high that the tin soldier with one leg thought that *she* had only one leg too, like himself.

She would be the wife for me, he thought. *But she is very grand. She lives in a castle, and I have only a box.*

He watched her all the day, and was sure she sometimes looked at him. He determined to speak to her if ever he got the chance, for she really was the prettiest thing he had ever seen.

But alas! Misfortune came early to the tin soldier. The next morning the little boy placed him on the window ledge – and all at once the window blew open and out fell the little soldier head over heels to the pavement. He stuck head downwards there, his helmet and bayonet between the paving stones.

The little boy came out to look for him, but he could not find him, even though once he nearly trod on him.

Soon it began to rain, and the soldier lay there getting wetter and wetter. When the shower was over, two boys came by, and spied the tin soldier on the pavement.

'Just look!' cried one. 'There lies a tin soldier! Let's make him a paper boat and sail him down the gutter!'

So they made a boat out of newspaper, put the tin soldier in the middle of it, and let him sail away down the gutter while they ran beside him, clapping their hands for joy.

But, oh, dear! How the waves rose in that gutter, and how fast the stream ran! The paper boat rocked up and down, and sometimes turned round so fast that the tin soldier trembled; but he stuck fast, looked straight before him, and shouldered his gun bravely.

All at once the boat went into a long drain, and it became very dark.

Suddenly there came a great rat, which chased after the boat. 'Stop him, stop him!' cried the rat. 'I'll have him; I'll have him! What does he mean by coming along my drain?'

The stream became stronger and stronger, and carried the boat quickly away from the fierce rat. The water was running swiftly to a canal, and the poor tin soldier could hear the rush of the water as he got near to where the drain entered the canal. He felt very much frightened, but he didn't move an eyebrow. He remembered that he was a soldier and must never show fear.

His paper boat was getting fuller and fuller. At last it was so full that the water stood right up to his neck and he felt sure that in another moment he would be drowned. Then with a swirl and a rush he was swept right out into the canal, his boat sank and the waters closed over his head.

Now I shall surely drown! thought the little tin soldier.

But at that very moment he was snapped up by a great fish! Oh, how dark it was in that fish's body! And so narrow too. But the brave tin soldier lay unmoved there, never showing for a moment how very much afraid he was.

The fish swam to and fro. He made the most wonderful movements, and then he suddenly became quite still. At last something flashed through him like lightning. The daylight shone through, and a voice said aloud, 'Why, a tin soldier! He has been swallowed by the fish!'

The fish had been caught, carried to market, bought and taken into the kitchen, where the cook cut him open with a large knife. She seized the soldier, and carried him upstairs to the nursery to show the children what a find she had made.

'He is quite a hero!' she said, and placed him on the table for the children to see.

They bent over to see the wonderful little fellow who had had such an adventure. Then one of the boys gave a cry, and stretched out his hand to the soldier.

'Why!' he said. 'It is one of my own tin soldiers! It is the one I lost this morning! I should always know him again because he has only one leg! What a brave little fellow he is, to tumble from the window, get into the canal, be swallowed by a fish and then brought here again! He is a real hero. I shall not put him back into the box with the others. He shall go and live in the castle with the little dancing doll!'

The tin soldier could hardly believe his good luck when he heard this! Of all the things in the world this was the one he wanted the most. Now he would be able to talk to the little doll, and make friends with her.

So he was put in the castle, and stood at the door with the little lady, and a very fine pair they made, I can tell you. As for the dainty dancer, she was very pleased to have such a hero with her in the castle.

And there they stand now, looking at each other proudly, longing for the night to come, when they can talk to each other and say all that they want to. And I shouldn't be a bit surprised to hear that all the toys are bidden to go to a wedding soon, for if ever a pair were suited to each other I am sure it is the little lady and the brave tin soldier!

The Strange Tale
of the Unicorn

The Strange Tale
of the Unicorn

LONG AGO there was a village called Roundy because all the houses were built round a big ring of green grass. The houses were round too, and it really was the funniest little place you ever saw.

All the houses had people living in them except one tiny round cottage, which had only one living room and one bedroom in it. Nobody wanted to live there because the chimney smoked dreadfully, the walls were damp and there were hundreds and hundreds of black beetles living in the kitchen. So the little round house stood empty for many a year.

Then one day a strange creature came to Roundy

Village. It was a unicorn! You must have seen pictures of them, horse-like creature with one long horn sticking right out from the centre of their foreheads. The people flocked to see the strange animal and the children pointed their fingers at it and asked what it was.

On its back it carried three great bundles, and it looked all round the little village as it passed through. And suddenly it saw the empty cottage!

It walked up to the little broken gate and opened it. It peered in at the windows, and then pushed the door open and went inside.

'This will do for me!' said the unicorn in a deep voice. 'Two rooms are just enough!'

So the unicorn settled down to live in the cottage all by himself. He undid his bundles with his hooves and spread them out. There was a table, a bed, two chairs, pots and pans and a few dishes. Not very much to furnish a house with, but his cottage was so small that even those few things seemed to fill it.

'It's dirty,' said the unicorn, looking round. 'I must get someone in to clean it. The walls are damp too. I must get some wood and light a big fire.'

He went to the next cottage and knocked at the door. Mrs Dimple had quite a fright when she opened it and saw the unicorn standing there.

'Can you tell me where I can get someone to come in and clean for me?' asked the unicorn politely.

'Dear me, you're not really going to live next door, are you?' asked Mrs Dimple in surprise. 'Fancy a unicorn living in a cottage!'

'Well, why not?' said the unicorn. 'I must live somewhere! Come, tell me who will clean my house for me?'

'Do you see that cottage painted white over there?' asked Mrs Dimple, pointing across the green grass. 'Well, Dame Hobble lives there with her daughter and stepdaughter. One of them will be sure to clean up for you.'

'Thank you,' said the unicorn and went to call at the

white-painted cottage. Dame Hobble opened the door and gaped at him in surprise. But when she heard that he had plenty of money and would pay well for his cleaning she stopped staring at him and called Melia, her daughter.

'Melia will clean for you,' she said. 'Won't you, Melia?'

Melia looked sulky. She hated cleaning – but when her mother whispered to her that she would be very well paid for her work she said yes, she would go and clean up the cottage for the unicorn.

'Come tomorrow,' said the unicorn and went back to his cottage.

'Now mind you clean well for him,' said Melia's mother to her pouting daughter. 'He's rich.'

'I don't like working for a silly old unicorn,' sulked Melia. 'Why can't Susan go?'

'Well, do you want Susan to get the money for it then?' asked her mother.

'Let us go together, and I'll make her do most of

the work,' said Melia artfully. 'We can give her a little of the money, Mother, but I'll see that she does nearly all the work!'

'Very well,' said her mother, who hated Susan, her pretty stepdaughter, and was quite willing that she should go and do most of the work for a tiny part of the money.

So the next day the two girls went across the green to the unicorn's cottage. Susan had on a strong overall, and carried a bucket, soap, cloths and brushes with her. Melia hadn't even troubled to put on an apron and all she carried was a duster. The unicorn opened the door. Melia giggled at the sight of him, but Susan looked into his deep brown eyes and wondered why they seemed so unhappy.

The two girls set to work – at least Susan began to scrub the floors and wash the walls, while Melia wandered about prying into the cupboards and drawers. The unicorn caught her peeping and spoke to her sharply, and she answered him rudely. He looked at her so strangely that she took up her duster and began to rub the windows with it.

Susan worked hard all that week. She made the floor shine and windows glitter, the fireplace bright and all the furniture gleam like mirrors. Melia only gave her twopence a day out of the money that the unicorn handed her, but she did not dare to complain.

Week after week Melia and Susan went to cook and clean for the unicorn. Susan made him pretty curtains to hang at the windows. She caught a hedgehog and left it in the kitchen at nights to catch and eat all the hundreds of black beetles. She chopped up wood for his fire and even dug up his garden for him, for he could not do very much with hooves instead of hands.

Each week the unicorn paid out wages to Melia because she was the elder of the two, and each week Melia gave Susan only a few pence for all her work. The unicorn watched and wondered, but said nothing at all. Susan was always polite and kind to him, but

Melia was rough and rude. She thought it was strange for a unicorn to live in a house. Why didn't he live in a field and eat grass?

Then one week when Melia had burnt the cakes she had tried to make, upset a bowl of water on the floor and forgotten to mop it up, and stolen half of a fruit pie from the larder, the unicorn wouldn't give her any wages.

'No,' he said, 'you're a bad girl, Melia. You are lazy and do very little, and the little you do is always bad. Why should I give you the money? I am sure you don't give Susan her share. Here, Susan, take the money. You are not to give any of it to Melia. It is all for you. And in the future I don't want Melia to come and work for me, but only you.'

Well, Melia was so angry that she ran straight home to her mother and told her. When Susan got home they took the money from her and scolded her. Then they told her that she must go and work for the unicorn as he said, but every week they would take away her money.

'That will teach you to get into the silly unicorn's good books and push Melia out of them!' said her stepmother angrily.

Poor Susan! She was very miserable. She went to work for the unicorn as usual, but every week all her money was taken away and she was never allowed even a penny for herself. Her clothes fell into rags and at last even the unicorn noticed how shabby and sad she looked.

'Why don't you buy yourself a new dress?' he asked. 'You get enough money, Susan. What do you do with it all?'

Susan didn't like to tell tales of her stepmother and stepsister. She went red and said nothing at all.

'Poor little Susan!' said the unicorn suddenly. 'Do they let you keep any of your money?'

Susan felt the tears coming into her eyes, and she wiped them away. The unicorn gave a heavy sigh, and she looked at him in surprise. His eyes were so sad that she couldn't bear to see them. She ran to him and flung her arms around his neck.

'Don't look like that!' she cried. 'I love you, dear kind unicorn. We are both unhappy, so let us comfort one another!'

She kissed the unicorn's velvety nose – and then sprang away in surprise. What was this? What was happening? Marvel of marvels, the unicorn no longer stood there, but a young prince with thick black locks and shining eyes.

'Susan! You kissed me and broke the spell! You loved me and destroyed the enchantment that made me a unicorn! I was changed into that strange shape by a wizard whom I accidentally knocked down when I was out riding. I was sad and unhappy, for none of my people knew me then, and I was forced to wander out into the world by myself, miserable and lonely.'

'A prince!' said Susan. 'Oh how wonderful – but, sir, forgive me for kissing you. I thought you were just a unicorn.'

'I shan't forgive you!' cried the prince, taking her into his arms and hugging her in delight. 'I'll only forgive you on one condition – come back with me to my palace and marry me!'

The prince sent a messenger to bring his carriage from his father's palace, and very soon there came not one carriage but many, all rolling into the little village of Roundy. The king and queen were in one, two princes and a princess in another, and a whole crowd of nobles followed. They were all overjoyed to hear from the prince again, for they had thought he was lost for ever.

'This is Susan who is going to marry me,' said the prince, and the king and queen kissed her lovingly. All the people of Roundy Village came out to see what was happening – and *how* Melia and her mother stared to see Susan climbing up into the king's own carriage with a handsome prince.

'Goodbye, Stepmother!' called Susan. 'The unicorn was really a prince and I'm going to marry him.'

How angry Melia was! She at once set out to find another unicorn and keep house for him. When he asked her to marry him she said yes – but, dear me, he wasn't a prince at all, but just an old, bad-tempered unicorn who did nothing but order her about from dawn till dusk. And a very good thing too!

Susan married her prince and, so the history books of that country say, they lived happily ever afterwards.

The Odd Little Bird

The Odd Little Bird

ONCE UPON a time there was a fine fat hen who was sitting on twelve eggs. Eleven of the eggs were brown but the twelfth was a funny greeny-grey colour. The hen didn't like it very much. She thought it must be a bad egg.

Still, she thought to herself, *I'll see if it hatches out with the others. If it doesn't, well, it will show it is a bad egg.*

After many days the hen was sure her eggs were going to hatch.

'I can hear a little "Cheep cheep" in one of them!' she clucked excitedly to all the other hens. Sure enough one of the eggs cracked, and out came a fluffy yellow chick, who cuddled up in the mother hen's feathers with a cheep of joy.

Then one by one all the other eggs cracked too, and tiny fluffy birds crept out – all except the greeny-grey egg. No chick came from that. It lay there in the nest unhatched.

'Well, I'll give it another day or two,' said the hen, sitting down on it again. 'After that I won't sit on it any more.'

In two days the hen found that the twelfth egg was cracking too. Out came a small bird – but it wasn't a bit like the other chicks!

It was yellow certainly – but its beak was bigger and quite different. Its body was different too, and the little creature waddled about clumsily instead of running with the others.

The mother hen didn't like it. She pecked it and clucked. 'Oh, you funny-looking little thing! I'm sure you don't belong to me.'

The other chicks didn't like the little waddling

bird either. They called it names and shooed it away when it went to feed with them. It was sad and unhappy, for not even the mother hen welcomed it or called it to enjoy a titbit as she did the others.

'I'm the odd one,' it said to itself. 'I wonder why. I can't run fast like the others, and I don't look like them either. I am ugly and nobody wants me.'

The odd little bird grew faster than the others, and at last it was so much bigger that the little chicks didn't like to peck it any more, for they were afraid it might peck back and hurt them. So they left it alone, and stopped calling it names.

But the mother hen was not afraid of it. She was often very cross with it indeed, especially when the rain came and made puddles all over the hen run.

For then the odd little bird would cheep with delight and go splashing through the puddles in joy.

'You naughty, dirty little creature!' clucked the mother hen. 'Come back at once. No chicken likes its feet to be wet. You must be mad, you naughty little thing!'

Then the odd little bird would be well pecked by the hen, and would sit all by itself in a corner, watching the rain come down and wishing it could go out in it.

One day it found a hole in the hen run and crept through it. Not far off it saw a piece of water, and on it were some lovely white birds, swimming about and making loud quacking noises. Something in the odd little bird's heart cried: 'Oh, if only I could be with those lovely birds, how happy I should be!'

But then it grew sad. 'No,' it said to itself, 'I am a queer, odd little bird. Nobody wants me. But all the same I will just go to the edge of the water and paddle my feet in it. I can run away if those big white birds chase me.'

So off it went and paddled in the water. It was lovely. At first the big white ducks took no notice of the little bird, and then two came swimming up quite near to him.

'Hallo!' they cried. 'What a little beauty you are! Come along with us and have a swim. We'd be proud to have you.'

At first the little bird didn't know that the ducks were talking to him. But when he saw that they really were, he was too astonished to answer. At last he found his voice, and said, 'But, lovely creatures, surely you don't want me, such an odd, ugly little bird as I am!'

'You're not odd or ugly,' cried the ducks. 'You are a beautiful little duck, like us. Come along, it is time you learnt to swim. Don't go back to those funny little chicks any more. Live with us, and have a fine swim on the water!'

The odd little bird could hardly believe what he heard. So he wasn't odd or ugly after all! He was only different from the chicks because he was a duckling! And he would grow up to be like these lovely white creatures, and swim with them on the water. Oh, what happiness!

'Quack, quack!' he said, for the first time, and swam

boldly out to join the ducks. The old mother hen spied him through the hole in the run and squawked to him to come back. But he waggled his tail and laughed.

'No, no!' he cried. 'You will never make a hen of me. I'm a duck, a duck, a duck!'

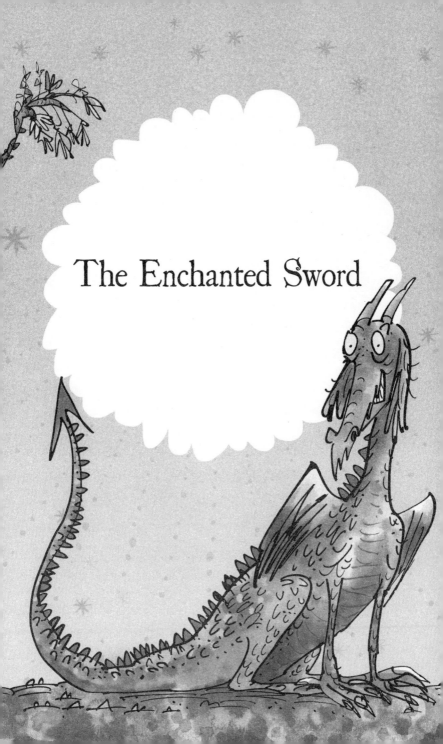

The Enchanted Sword

The Enchanted Sword

THERE ONCE lived a king called Uther Pendragon, who loved the fair Igraine of Cornwall. She did not return his love, and Uther fell ill with grief.

As he lay on his bed, Merlin the magician appeared before him.

'I know what sorrow is in your heart,' he said to the king. 'If you will promise what I ask, I will, by my magic art, give you Igraine for your wife.'

'I will grant you all you ask,' said Uther. 'What do you wish?'

'As soon as you and Igraine have a baby son, will you give him to me?' asked Merlin. 'Nothing but good shall come to the child, I promise you.'

'So be it,' said the king. 'Give me Igraine for my wife, and you shall have my first son.'

It came to pass as Merlin promised. The fair Igraine became Uther Pendragon's wife, and made him very happy. One night a baby son was born to her and the king and Uther looked upon the child's face, and was grieved when he remembered his promise to Merlin.

He named the tiny boy Arthur, and then commanded that he should be taken down to the postern gate, wrapped in a cloth of gold.

'At the gate you will see an old man. Give the child to him,' said the king to two of his knights. The knights did as they were commanded, and delivered the baby to Merlin, who was waiting at the postern gate.

The magician took the child to a good knight called Sir Ector, and the knight's wife welcomed the baby, and tended him lovingly, bringing him up as if he were her own dear son.

THE ENCHANTED SWORD

Not very long after this King Uther fell ill and died. Then many mighty lords wished to be king and fought one another, so that the kingdom was divided against itself and could not stand against any foe.

There came a day when Merlin the magician rode to the Archbishop of Canterbury and bade him command all the great lords of the land to come to London by Christmas and worship in the church there.

'There shall you know who is to be king of this country,' said Merlin, 'for a great marvel shall be shown you.'

So the archbishop sent for all the lords and knights, commanding them to come to the church in London by Christmas, and they obeyed.

When the people came out of church a cry of wonder was heard – for there, in the churchyard, was a great stone, and in the middle of it was an anvil of steel a foot high. In the anvil was thrust a beautiful sword, and round it, written in letters of gold upon the stone, were these words:

Who so pulleth out this sword from this stone and anvil is rightwise king born of all England.

Lords and knights pressed round the sword and marvelled to see it thrust into the stone, for neither sword nor stone had been there when they went into the church.

Then many men caught hold of the sword and tried to pull it forth, but could not. Try as they would, they could not move it an inch. It was held fast, and not even the strongest knight there could draw it forth.

'The man is not here that shall be king of this realm,' said the archbishop. 'Set ten men to guard the stone day and night. Then, when New Year's Day is come, we will hold a tournament, and the bravest and strongest in the kingdom shall joust one with another. Mayhap by that time there shall come the one who will draw forth the sword and be hailed as king of this fair land.'

Now, when New Year's Day came, many lords and

knights rode on the field to take part in the tournament. With them went the good knight Sir Ector, to whom Merlin had given the baby Arthur some years before.

Sir Ector had brought up the boy with his own son, Sir Kay, and had taught him all the arts of knighthood, so that he grew up brave and courteous. He loved Sir Ector and his wife, and called them Father and Mother, for he thought that they were truly his parents. Sir Kay he thought was his brother, and he was glad and proud that Kay, who had been made knight only a few months before, should be going to joust at the tournament.

Sir Ector, Sir Kay and Arthur set off to go to the lists. On the way there Sir Kay found that his sword, which he had unbuckled the night before, had been left at the house. He had forgotten it!

'I pray you, Arthur, ride back to the house and fetch me my sword,' he said to the boy beside him.

'Willingly!' answered Arthur, and turning his horse's head round, he rode swiftly back to fetch Kay's sword. But when he got to the house he found the door locked, for all the women had gone to see the tournament.

Then Arthur was angry and dismayed, for he knew how disappointed his brother would be if he returned without his sword.

'I will ride to the churchyard, and take the sword from the stone there,' he said to himself. 'My brother Kay shall not be without a sword this day!'

So when he came to the churchyard, Arthur leapt off his horse and tied it to a post. Then he went to ask the men who guarded the sword if he might take it. But they were not there, for they too had gone to the tournament.

Then the boy ran to the stone, and took hold of the handle of the sword. He pulled at it fiercely, and – lo and behold! – it came forth from the steel anvil, and shone brightly in the sunshine.

Arthur leapt on to his horse once again, and rode to Kay.

'Here is a sword for you, brother,' he said.

Sir Kay took the beautiful weapon, and looked at it in amazement, for he knew at once that it was the sword from the stone. He ran to his father and showed it to him.

'Where did you get it?' asked Sir Ector in astonishment and awe.

'My brother Arthur brought it to me,' answered Sir Kay.

'Sir, I will tell you all,' said Arthur, fearing that he had done wrong. 'When I went back for Kay's sword I found the door locked. So, lest my brother should be without a weapon this day, I rode to the churchyard and took the sword from the great stone there.'

'Then you must be king of this land,' said Sir Ector, 'for so say the letters around the anvil. Come with me to the churchyard, and you shall put the sword in the stone again and I will see you draw it forth.'

The three rode to the church, and Arthur thrust the sword into the anvil, then drew it forth again easily and lightly. Then he put it back, and Sir Ector strove to draw it forth and could not. After him Sir Kay tried, but he could not so much as stir it an inch.

Then once again Arthur pulled it forth, and at that both Sir Ector and Sir Kay fell down upon their knees before him.

'Why do you kneel to me?' asked the boy. 'My father and my brother, why is this?'

'Nay, nay,' said Sir Ector. 'We are not your father and your brother. Long years ago the magician Merlin brought you to us as a baby, and we took you and nursed you, not knowing who you were.'

Then Arthur began to weep, for he was sad to hear that the man and woman he loved so much were not his parents, and that Kay was not his brother. But Sir Ector comforted him, and took him to the archbishop, bidding him tell how he had drawn forth the enchanted sword.

Then once again Arthur was bidden to ride to the churchyard, this time accompanied by all the lords and knights. He thrust the sword into the stone, and then pulled it forth. At that many lords came round the stone, shouting that what a mere boy could do could be done by a man with ease.

But when they tried to draw forth the sword, they could not. Each man had his turn, and failed. Then, before all the watching people, Arthur lightly drew out the sword, and flourished it around his head.

'We will have Arthur for our king!' shouted the people. 'Let us crown him! He is our king, and we will have none other!'

Then they all knelt before him, and begged the archbishop to anoint him as king.

So, when the right time came, Arthur was crowned, and swore to be a true king and to rule with justice all the days of his life.

A Lovely Welcome Home

A Lovely
Welcome Home

ONCE UPON a time the fairy queen had worked so hard that the king had to take her away to stay by the Dream Sea. She was so dreadfully tired that he kept her there all the summer.

'But what will all my fairies do without me to help them?' she kept saying.

'Never mind that,' said the king. 'They must get on somehow or other, and you must have a long rest.'

Of course all the fairies in Fairyland missed her very much. It seemed very strange not to have someone in the palace who was always ready to listen to them, or to see what work they were doing.

'When is our queen coming back?' they asked the palace fairies.

'She is coming back in *two* weeks,' they answered joyfully. 'We had a letter this morning, brought by a peacock butterfly.'

'Hurray! Hurray!' shouted the fairies, and they flew off all over Fairyland, as fast as they could, to spread the good news.

'We must do something lovely to welcome her home again,' said the chief fairies. 'We'll hold a great meeting about it.'

So a meeting was held in the biggest hall of the palace, and hundreds and hundreds of fairies came.

'The queen is coming home through the green beech wood, along the blackberry lanes, through the dewy field, and then up the palace gardens,' said the Lord High Chamberlain of Fairyland.

'We will polish all our dewdrops most beautifully, and hang them on the grasses,' said the fairies who lived in the dewy field.

'And we'll go and ask the blackberries to grow very black and sweet, so that when the queen comes along she may pick some for herself,' cried the lane fairies, flying off at once.

'The rose trees will grow their very best roses,' said the palace gardeners joyfully, 'and perhaps the dear queen will pick one for her buttonhole.'

'See that a glorious supper is prepared for Her Majesty,' commanded the Lord High Chamberlain, turning to the fairy cooks.

'Oh, yes, yes, yes!' cried the cooks. 'We'll make a big sugar cake, shaped just like a castle, and a pudding with jam on top and ice cream underneath!'

Only the wood fairies said nothing.

'What will *you* do to welcome back the queen?' asked the Lord High Chamberlain.

'We don't know,' they answered sadly. 'The trees have lost their beautiful fresh spring green, and they look tired and dark, now it's autumn.'

'Couldn't you brighten them up a bit?' asked

the chamberlain. 'Why don't you hang some flags on them?'

'Oh, they wouldn't like that,' said the wood fairies. 'But we'll go and ask them.'

Off they flew to the beech wood.

They told the trees that the queen was coming home in two weeks, and made them most excited about it. They waved their branches about as they talked.

'What *can* we do to welcome her back?' they asked.

'I've got an idea,' suddenly said a wood fairy, 'but I don't know if you'd like it.'

'Tell us,' begged the beech trees.

'Well, you're dusty and dark green now,' said the fairy, 'but if you'd let us paint you a gay colour, you'd look lovely.'

'Oh, do, do,' said all the trees.

'Oh, I don't think we could do that,' said the chief fairy. 'The paint would make your leaves look lovely, but it might kill them too, and make them drop off.'

'We wouldn't mind, even if it hurt us,' said all the

trees. 'We love the queen, and we'd do anything to make things beautiful when she came home.'

'All right,' answered the wood fairies. 'We'll go and get some gold-brown paint for you.'

They flew off at once and mixed some beautiful gold-brown paint. They told the lane fairies what they were going to do with it.

'What a splendid idea!' they said. 'We'll ask the blackberries if they'd like their leaves painted red. We are sure they would.'

The idea spread all through the woods and lanes and hedges. The wood fairies were very busy. They sat up in the beech trees and painted every leaf a lovely golden brown. The lane fairies made the blackberry brambles perfectly beautiful with red leaves – and all the other trees, oak, hawthorn and elm, begged to be painted too.

On the day that the queen was expected home Fairyland looked simply glorious. The beech wood was a waving glory of gold; the other trees shone red, brown or yellow; and as for the creeper over the palace wall, well, it almost made you blink to look at it, it was such a brilliant red!

As the queen journeyed home she could hardly believe her eyes!

'What *has* happened to all the trees?' she cried. 'How beautiful they are! What *have* the wood fairies been doing?'

'They've painted our leaves,' whispered the trees proudly.

'But that will soon make your leaves fall off,' said the queen.

'They'll grow again in the spring,' answered the trees, as one of the gold-brown leaves fluttered down for the queen to tread on. 'And *we* don't mind, if only you're pleased and happy.'

'Oh, it's a *lovely* homecoming!' cried the queen. 'And everything does look so wonderfully beautiful. Don't you think we could always make things look like this in the autumn?'

'Yes, let's,' cried all the fairies, and all the trees. 'We'd *love* to!'

So every year now, directly the autumn comes, the beeches and the blackberry bushes, the oaks and the creepers, are all painted in gold and brown, red, yellow and orange, just as they were ages ago when the fairy queen was welcomed home from the Dream Sea.

Little Red
Riding Hood

Little Red Riding Hood

ONCE UPON a time there was a pretty little girl with golden hair. She was good to her mother, and often helped her with the housework and the mending.

She always wore a dear little red cap, and everyone called her 'Little Red Riding Hood'.

One day her mother spoke to her. 'Put a cake and a pot of cream into your basket, and take them to your grandmother, who lives in the wood.'

Little Red Riding Hood put the cake and the cream into her basket and ran out of the door. 'Listen!' cried her mother. 'Be sure to go straight to your granny's and back! Do not stop to play on the way, and do NOT talk to the wolf. He is wicked and sly.'

'Don't worry, Mother!' called Red Riding Hood.
'I shall soon be back.'

Then she went on her way through the woods,
singing a merry little song.

Soon she came to a woodcutter, and he called to her.
'Well, little girl, where are you off to this fine day?'

'I am taking my granny a cake and some cream,'
said Little Red Riding Hood.

'Beware of the wolf then,' said the woodcutter,
'and do not listen to anything he says!'

Little Red Riding Hood ran gaily through the
bushes. She picked some bright toadstools and a
bunch of wild flowers, singing merrily all the time.

Then suddenly there came a wolf, with a sharp nose
and long ears. Red Riding Hood screamed, but the
wolf spoke gently to her. 'Good day, my dear little
girl, are you out for a walk?'

'Yes, Mr Wolf, I am going to see my granny.'

'Shall we have a little race?' went on the wolf,

'and see who reaches your granny's house first? You shall go that way and I will go this.'

The wolf took a short cut and came to the cottage very quickly. Rat-a-tat! Rat-a-tat! He knocked at the door, but nobody answered. 'The cottage is empty,' said the wolf. 'I will go in!'

The wolf went inside the cottage and looked around. 'I have a good idea!' he said. 'I will find some of the old granny's clothes. Now, where will they be?'

He soon found some in a chest of drawers, and quickly dressed himself.

He put on a long white nightdress, and tied the blue ribbons under his hairy chin.

'I look just like a very, very old dame,' he said. 'Little Red Riding Hood will think I am her granny!'

The wolf climbed into bed, pulled the sheets right up to his chin, and then put on the old granny's glasses. 'Aha!' he said. 'No one would guess I am an old wolf now. Hurry, Red Riding Hood, come quickly!'

Little Red Riding Hood played with the birds and listened to their songs – and then she saw that the sun was setting! 'Oh, I shall be late!' she cried. 'I must go to my granny's!' and she ran off quickly.

At last she came to the little cottage. The door was fast shut, and she knocked. Rat-a-tat-tat!

'Who is there?' called a voice. 'Your little granddaughter!' answered Red Riding Hood. 'I bring you a cake and some cream.'

'Come in, my child!' said the voice. 'Come in!'

The little girl went into the cottage. 'Oh, Granny!' she said. 'You are in bed – are you ill?'

'Yes, I am ill,' said the wolf. 'Come close to me so that I can see you and hear you easily.' The wolf hid himself as well as he could under the bedclothes, and pulled the bonnet well over his head.

'Granny, what big ears you have!' said Red Riding Hood.

'All the better to hear you with!'

'What big eyes you have!'

'All the better to see you with!'

'And, Granny, what big teeth you have!'

'All the better to *eat* you with!' cried the wolf.

He leapt out of bed and pounced on the frightened little girl, but his feet caught in the long nightdress, and he could not catch Little Red Riding Hood. She ran out of the door, shouting, 'Help! Help!'

A woodcutter was just passing by and heard her calls. He took a big stick and struck the wicked wolf, who fell down and died.

The little girl's granny, who had been out searching for firewood, heard the cries and the shouts, and came running up. She was just in time to see the bad wolf being carried away.

Then the granny took the frightened little girl into her cottage and sat her on her knee. 'You must never, never listen to any wolf,' she said. 'And you must never, never stop to play when you are sent on an errand. Now, dry your tears – we will have tea together, and then I will take you safely home!'

The Dragon Called
Snap

The Dragon Called Snap

THERE WAS once upon a time a dragon called Snap. You can guess why he had that name. It was because when he took anything into his mouth he snapped it up and his mouth shut with a smack. He lived all alone on the side of a steep hill, and people were very much afraid of him.

Now Snap was very lonely. He was a kindly dragon, and he had never had any wish to eat people, but liked best of all a meal of fresh young dandelions or nice new daisy leaves. He liked to eat these at night, and as he pulled them up his mouth went 'Snap! Snap! Snap!' and all the sleeping people down in the village below awoke and shivered with fright.

One day Snap was so lonely that he made up his mind to walk down to the village and make friends with the people there. So off he started. Down the hill he went and soon came to the school, where the children were doing their lessons, just as you do. Imagine their enormous surprise when they looked up and saw the dragon staring in at their classroom window! They were not frightened because the dragon looked so kindly at them and opened his mouth to smile. When he shut it, it went 'Snap!' again, and the teacher felt she had really better give the alarm. So she rang the school fire bell, and that sent all the mothers and fathers flying to the school to see if their children were safe.

My goodness me, when they saw the dragon, what a fright they were in! They rang bells and banged saucepan lids to frighten him, and very soon the startled creature was racing back to his hill as fast as ever he could, disappointed and sad.

He sat down by his cave that night and began to cry. 'Wow!' he went. 'Wow! Wow-ow-ow!' He had an enormous voice, and he woke up a goblin who lived deep inside the hill. The goblin lit a candle and, most annoyed, went to see what was the matter. He fell into the stream of water made by the dragon's tears, and that made him crosser than ever.

'Whatever are you making that terrible noise for?' asked the goblin, holding up the candle to see the dragon.

'I want to g-g-g-go and l-l-live with the v-v-village people!' wept the dragon dismally.

'Well,' said the goblin, putting down his candle and feeling in his pockets, 'I've just the thing for you. You swallow this, Dragon, and I'll take you down to the village tomorrow. I'll put you into somebody's garden, and, you'll see, they will be so happy to have you!'

The dragon was delighted. He obediently swallowed the pill that the goblin gave him – and, my goodness, how queer he felt! He grew smaller and smaller and smaller, and his tail seemed to root itself into the hillside. The goblin took a look at him and chuckled.

'Ha ha!' he said. 'You won't wake me up any more with your silly wailing and crying, Dragon!'

In the morning the goblin went to where the dragon had been and pulled up a small plant – all that was left of the poor dragon. He popped it into his pocket and went down to the village. He planted it in somebody's garden and left it.

It grew, and it grew. People found it and loved it. It was a funny little plant, and it had a mouth that you could open. It snapped back shut each time, so what do you suppose people called it? Guess! Yes. Snapdragon, of course, although they never once guessed how right they were!

The Biscuit Tree

The Biscuit Tree

ONCE THERE was a brownie called Mickle who was very poor. He lived in a tumbledown cottage, and grew potatoes and cabbages in his garden, and nothing else, because it was so small.

But though he was poor he was as kind as could be. If anyone came knocking at his yellow front door begging for a penny, he would shake his head and say, 'I haven't even a ha'penny. But you may have a slice of bread, or two or three potatoes.'

If anyone wanted help, Mickle would always run to give it. When old Dame Fanny broke her leg he went in to sweep and dust her cottage every day, and he fed her hens so well that they laid even more eggs than usual.

And when Mr Winkle had his roof blown off in a storm, Mickle took a ladder and spent the whole day mending Winkle's roof most beautifully.

Most people knew how to reward Mickle for his kindness. They would give him a few biscuits.

Mickle was so poor that he never bought a biscuit for himself. His meals were mostly bread, potato and cabbage, sometimes with soup for a treat.

And he did love biscuits so much!

'I really don't know which biscuits I love most,' he would say. 'The gingersnaps are marvellous – such a lovely taste. And the chocolate biscuits that Dame Fanny makes simply melt in my mouth. And as for those little biscuits with the jam in the middle, well, I could eat them all day long!'

Now one day Mickle had a bit of bad luck. A goat got into his garden and ate all his winter cabbages! And when he went to his sack of potatoes to help himself to one or two, he found that a rat must have told his family about them, for nearly all had disappeared through a hole at one end of the sack!

Mickle could have cried! All his winter greens gone – and most of his potatoes! What was he to live on now?

He went indoors. He had been to help Pixie Lightfoot to dig her garden that day, and she had given him six pat-a-cake biscuits as a reward. He had meant to keep them for Sundays, and eat one each Sunday for six weeks at teatime. But today he was so hungry that he felt he could eat them all!

Now just outside at that very moment was a little child. Her father was travelling through the village. She was tired and cold, and when she saw the smoke rising from Mickle's chimney she thought it would be very nice just to peep inside the door and look at the fire.

So, as Mickle was about to take a bite from the first biscuit, he saw the door slowly open, and the untidy curly head of the little child come peeping round the corner!

Mickle stared in surprise. The child smiled and came right in.

'I'm cold,' she said. 'I saw the smoke coming from your chimney and I wanted to look at a nice warm fire.'

'Come and sit down by it,' said Mickle at once. 'It's only made of sticks from the woods, but it is cheerful and warm.'

So the little girl sat down and warmed her hands. She looked at the bag that Mickle was holding and asked him what was inside it.

'Biscuits,' said Mickle.

'Ooh!' said the child, but she didn't ask for one. Her eyes grew rounder, and she looked small and hungry. Mickle felt that he simply *must* give her a biscuit. So he handed her one.

'Thank you!' said the girl, and crunched it up as quickly as a dog eats a bone! Then she looked hungrily at the bag again.

Mickle knew he shouldn't give her any more because he wouldn't have any for the next five Sundays. But he found his hand going inside the bag, and there it was, holding out another biscuit again!

Well, the girl ate five of those six biscuits, and Mickle was just handing her the very last one, when there came a shout from the gate, 'Hi, Annie, hi! Where are you? Come along at once!'

The child jumped up. Her name was Annie, and it was her father who was calling her. She gave Mickle a quick hug and flew out into the garden. Her father was standing by the gate, waiting.

'This brownie man has been so kind to me, Father!' cried the little girl. 'Give him a reward. Please do!'

She bit her last biscuit and some crumbs fell to the ground beside the gate. Her father trod them into the earth with his foot and muttered a few strange words. He looked at Mickle out of bright green eyes.

'Sometimes a bit of kindness grows and grows and

brings us a reward we don't expect!' he said. 'And sometimes it doesn't! But today there is magic in the wind, so maybe you'll be lucky!'

He nodded to Mickle and he and the child went dancing up the lane together, their clothes blowing like dead leaves in the wind. Mickle shut the gate and went back to his warm kitchen. He was hungry – and all his biscuits were gone. Life was very sad.

He forgot all about the man and his daughter that spring. He never saw them again, and he worked so hard that he really hadn't time to think of anything except food and rest and work.

But one day he noticed a strong little shoot growing by his gatepost. He bent down to look at it. It was not like any seedling he had seen before. Perhaps it was a weed. Mickle thought he would pull it up. Then he thought he wouldn't. So he left it.

And to his enormous surprise it grew and grew very fast indeed, till in three weeks' time it was as high as the top of his gate! It sprouted into leaves.

It grew higher still. It grew into a small tree, and Mickle had to walk under it when he went out of the gate. It was really most extraordinary!

He talked to his friends about it. They were used to magic, of course, but no one had ever seen a tree grow quite so quickly.

'It will flower soon and then we shall know what it is,' said his friends. And the next week, sure enough, it did flower. It had funny flowers – bright red, with flat yellow middles.

The blossoms didn't last long. The red petals fell off, and the flat yellow middles grew larger. Everyone was most puzzled – till at last Dame Fanny gave a shout and slapped Mickle suddenly on the shoulder.

'It's a biscuit tree! That's what it is! A biscuit tree! Goodness me, one hasn't grown in the kingdom for about five hundred years! A biscuit tree, a biscuit tree!'

Well, Dame Fanny was right. It was a biscuit tree, and no mistake! The biscuits grew till they were ripe, and a sort of sugary powder came over them. Then they were ready for picking.

And how Mickle enjoyed picking biscuits off his biscuit tree! You would have loved it too. He got some big and little tins from his grocer, lined them with paper, and then picked the biscuits. He laid each one neatly in a tin, till the tin was full and he could put the lid on. Then he took up another tin and filled that. He did enjoy himself.

He gave a tin of biscuits to everyone in the village. This was just like kind old Mickle, of course. They were pat-a-cake biscuits, and for a long time nobody knew why the tree was a pat-a-cake biscuit tree, nor why it had grown at all. And then Pixie Lightfoot suddenly remembered that she had given Mickle some pat-a-cake biscuits some months back.

'What did you do with them?' she asked Mickle. 'Did you eat them?'

'No,' said Mickle. 'I gave them all to a child.'

'Did she drop any crumbs near your gate, where the biscuit tree is growing?' asked Lightfoot.

'Yes – she did – and, I remember now, her father stamped them into the ground, and said that sometimes kindness grew its own reward – and he said that there was magic in the wind that day!' cried Mickle.

'Ah, now we know everything!' said Lightfoot. 'It was your own bit of kindness that grew! From the biscuit crumbs came your wonderful tree, Mickle. Oh, how marvellous! I do hope it goes on flowering year after year.'

Well, it does, of course, so Mickle always has plenty of biscuits to eat, sell or give away. Go by his gate in Misty Village during the summer and see his biscuits growing on the tree – he'll be sure to give you a pocketful if you wish him good morning!

Mr Fee-Fie-Fo

Mr Fee-Fie-Fo

PEGGY AND John lived not very far away from Fee-Fie-Fo Wood. It wasn't a very nice wood because it was damp and dark, and in the very middle of it lived old Mr Fee-Fie-Fo and his wife.

Every day when they went to school their mother said the same thing to them.

'Now mind you don't set foot in Fee-Fie-Fo Wood or old Mr Fee-Fie-Fo may get you.'

And every day Peggy and John gave her the same answer. 'No, Mother, we won't.'

One day they disobeyed. John had a lovely new ball and he and Peggy were playing with it. Peggy missed it and, oh, dear, off it went rolling into Fee-Fie-Fo Wood.

'There!' said John crossly. 'You've lost it.'

'We'll get it,' said Peggy. 'It's only gone a little way into the wood. Mr Fee-Fie-Fo won't see us!'

So the two children jumped over the ditch that separated the path from the wood and began to hunt for their ball. Suddenly they heard a noise and they looked up.

Oh, goodness me, it was old Mr Fee-Fie-Fo! He was a tall, thin man, and he wore a yellow top hat and a green smock. His boots were red, and he had a beard that came halfway down his green smock.

'Ho!' he said, rubbing his hands. 'So you've come into my wood, have you? Well, just come a little further, my bold children! I'm wanting someone to help me with my magic spells and you'll do very well indeed.'

He caught up the two scared children and carried them off. After some time he came to a higgledy-piggledy cottage, and at the gate stood his wife, a large woman with tiny eyes.

'Here are two children to help me with my spells,' said Mr Fee-Fie-Fo. 'Lock them up in my magic room and get ready for the cat spell. I'll be along in an hour.'

Mrs Fee-Fie-Fo took the two children to a queer room at the back of the cottage and locked them in there with her. It was a very strange room. There was a big fire at one end and on it boiled an iron cauldron. Green smoke came from it, and it sang a magic song to itself.

On the floor were many circles and squares, and up the walls grew strange plants in pots. There was one big window but it was barred. There could be no escape that way.

'What is this cat spell that Mr Fee-Fie-Fo wants us to help him with?' asked John. 'Will he let us go when we have helped him?'

'He may do,' said the woman. 'But you'll be turned

into cats, you know, so you'll have to be careful not to go near any dogs in case they chase you. I hope you won't mind being turned into cats.'

'I couldn't bear it!' said Peggy, beginning to cry. 'Oh, do let us go.'

'I couldn't possibly do that,' said the old dame. 'Why, Mr Fee-Fie-Fo would be dreadfully cross with me.'

She began to get ready for the cat spell. First of all she rubbed out some of the circles on the floor, and then drew two little ones. She told the children to stand inside them.

Then she went to the cauldron and stirred it. She took a jar of golden honey and emptied it into the iron pot, and she threw six hairs from a cat into it too. Then she opened a cupboard nearby and began hunting there.

'Oh, dear, oh, dear! Now wherever in the wide world can it have got to?' the children heard her say.

'What are you looking for?' asked John.

'I'm looking for my nutmeg grater,' said Mrs Fee-Fie-Fo, fussing about. 'I've got to grate a nutmeg into the cat spell, and I don't know where I've put the grater. Oh, yes – now I do remember! I broke it last Thursday! My goodness me, whatever shall I do? I simply *must* have a nutmeg grater!'

'Shall I go and borrow my mother's grater?' asked John. 'She's got a lovely big one, all new and shiny.'

'Well, that would be very, very kind of you,' said Mrs Fee-Fie-Fo. 'Now mind you don't take very long fetching it, or Fee-Fie-Fo won't find you when he's back again.'

She unlocked the door, and the two children tore out of the cottage. They raced down the path, panting, and did not stop for breath until they stood safely on the path outside Fee-Fie-Fo Wood.

'My goodness, what a narrow escape!' panted John. 'We'll never go into that wood again, Peggy. Thank goodness that old woman was so foolish!'

You can guess that neither of them jumped over the

ditch for a long time – but, would you believe it, there came a day when the children saw a brilliant yellow butterfly, and without thinking what they were doing they jumped over the ditch into Fee-Fie-Fo Wood and chased that butterfly.

And, of course, up came Mr Fee-Fie-Fo and caught them as easy as you please.

'Ho!' he said, smiling all over his bearded face. 'Ho! So I've got you again! Well, you won't escape *this* time! I want you for a frog spell today.'

'Oh, please don't turn us into frogs,' begged Peggy, but Mr Fee-Fie-Fo only laughed.

He took them home to his cottage and gave them to Mrs Fee-Fie-Fo.

'Tie them up to the leg of the kitchen table,' he said. 'Then they can't escape.'

He went out of the cottage, and left the children with his wife. She looked at them both.

'Dear, dear, if it isn't the naughty children who went off to fetch a nice shiny nutmeg grater for me, and never came back!' she said. 'Well, well, I must make sure you don't get away this time, mustn't I? I'll tie you up to the table leg as Fee-Fie-Fo said.'

She took down a tin and pulled out some string. It was very thin and John knew that he could easily break it. She tied them both up to the table leg, and then went on with her cooking.

Snap! John broke the string that tied him. Mrs Fee-Fie-Fo looked round.

'Oh, my, you've broken the string!' she said. 'Now, that is a nuisance, because you'll escape. I haven't any stronger string, so what shall I do? I think I'd better call Fee-Fie-Fo and tell him to get on with his frog spell at once.'

'No, don't do that,' said John. 'He might be cross with you. I'll tell you what I'll do. I'll go and get six-pennyworth of rope from the grocer's, and you may be sure no child can break *that*!'

'Does he sell *very* strong rope?' asked Mrs Fee-Fie-Fo.

'Very!' said Peggy and John together.

'Well, go and buy me some, but do be quick,' said the old dame.

Peggy broke the string that bound her, and once again the two children raced out of the cottage and ran to the ditch that lay between the wood and the path. How glad they were to find themselves safely on the path once more!

'We'll never, never do that again!' said John. And Peggy nodded her head, for she had no breath left to speak.

But, you know, they hadn't learnt their lesson yet – for in two months' time, when the wild strawberries were ripening, those silly children spied some very big ones just beyond the ditch. Over they jumped into Fee-Fie-Fo Wood, and they were soon eating them.

Mr Fee-Fie-Fo was watching for them. In a trice he had caught them, and was once again taking them to his higgledy-piggledy cottage. He gave them to his wife and told her to get them ready for the black-beetle spell.

Peggy was dreadfully frightened, because she didn't like beetles, and she thought it would be terrible to be one. She began to cry.

'And well you may cry!' said Mrs Fee-Fie-Fo, crossly. 'Wasn't it you two who ran off to buy me six-pennyworth of strong rope to tie you up with, and never came back? Well, you shan't escape this time, I tell you that for certain!'

She took them to the magic room and locked them there. The cauldron was still steaming with green smoke, and the chalk circles and squares were on the floor.

The old dame emptied this and that into the iron pot on the fire, and the green smoke changed first to red, then to yellow, and then to purple. It was all very strange indeed. The children were told to sit still on two black stools, and they didn't dare to move.

Mrs Fee-Fie-Fo made everything ready and then

she began to stir the cauldron with a red stick. While she stirred it she began to sing magic words. She spelt each word before she said it, and the children listened.

'S-h-o-o-n-a-r-o-o-n,' she spelt, then said the enchanted word, 'Shoonaroon. L-i-l-l-a-r-a-y, Lillaray, P-o-o-n-a . . .'

She suddenly stopped.

'Bother! I've forgotten how to spell Poonaskiltaree, a most important magic word in this spell. If I get it wrong the spell won't work. Do you know how to spell "Poonaskiltaree", children?'

'No,' said John. 'I've never heard of it before.'

'Dear, dear, dear,' said Mrs Fee-Fie-Fo in a flurry, stirring the cauldron so hard that the smoke changed to red again. 'I haven't a dictionary here to look it up in either. Whatever shall I do?'

'There's a dictionary at our school,' said John. 'Shall we go and fetch it for you?'

'Ho, ho!' said Mrs Fee-Fie-Fo with quite a clever look on her face. 'I know what you'll do! You'll run off and never come back again! No, no!'

'Well, let just one of us go and fetch it,' said John. 'Peggy knows where it is.'

'All right. Peggy shall get it,' said the old dame. 'But if she forgets to come back you'll certainly be turned into the blackest black beetle in the world, John.'

Peggy ran off at once, and John felt very glad to see her go. He didn't mind being made into a beetle if only Peggy escaped. Mrs Fee-Fie-Fo waited and waited, but Peggy didn't come back.

'Now whatever can she be doing?' said the old woman crossly.

'It's a very big, heavy dictionary,' said John. 'Perhaps she can't carry it. Shall I go and meet her and help her?'

'Yes, do,' said Mrs Fee-Fie-Fo. 'If she doesn't get here soon, old Fee-Fie-Fo will be back and we shan't be ready. Then goodness knows what will happen!'

Off ran John. How he raced through the wood!

And when he jumped over the ditch he found Peggy on the other side, waiting for him. She threw her arms round his neck and hugged him.

'Oh, John, I knew you'd escape somehow!' she said. 'We mustn't ever go into that horrid wood again! We really must be good obedient children and do what Mother says.'

I'm sure you will be glad to know that they have never jumped over that ditch again, and I hope they never will. As for Mr Fee-Fie-Fo, people do say he is still there, on the lookout for disobedient children – but others say he and his wife had a quarrel and turned one another into frogs. And I shouldn't be a bit surprised, would you?

Rapunzel

Rapunzel

ONCE UPON a time there lived a man and his wife in a little house near to a beautiful garden. The garden did not belong to them, but to an old witch, who would let none but herself walk there.

Although the woman could not go into the garden she could easily see into it whenever she sat at her bedroom window, for her window was higher than the very high wall that was all round the witch's garden.

The man and the woman longed for children, and the woman was always sighing because they had none.

One day she looked into the witch's garden and saw

some lettuce. It was very fresh and the edges were curly. It looked most delicious. The woman felt as if she really must have some lettuce like that to eat. So when her husband came home, she told him about it, and begged him to get her some from somewhere.

'There is no lettuce anywhere save in the witch's garden,' he told her.

'Get me some of that then!' begged the woman.

Now this was a dangerous thing to do, but the woman pined so much for the lettuce, and said she would be ill if she did not have it, that the man determined to get some for his wife that very night.

So when it was dark he climbed over the high wall and went to the lettuce bed. He pulled two big handfuls of the fresh green leaves, and then hurried back to his wife.

She ate it, and found it so good, that she begged him to get her some more on the next night. So the man climbed over a second time and went to the lettuce bed. But this time the old witch was on the watch for him, and she came limping towards him in a great rage.

'How dare you? How dare you?' she shouted in an angry voice. 'I grow those lettuces for myself, not for thieves!'

'Madam, forgive me!' begged the man. 'My wife was becoming ill for want of a salad, and there is none to be had save this in your garden.'

'Well, well, I will forgive you, if that is so,' said the witch. 'I have often seen your wife at the window and heard her sighing for a baby. If I forgive you, and let you go, will you promise me that if ever a baby comes to your wife, you will at once give it to me?'

The poor man did not dare to say no, so he promised. He went back to his wife and told her what the witch had said. She was very upset, but she could not scold her husband for making the promise, since it was her fault that he had been caught in the garden.

Soon after that a little baby girl was born to the man and his wife. They were delighted with her, and their grief was terrible when the witch walked in one day and reminded them of their promise. She picked up the baby and walked off with it, leaving the woman sobbing.

The baby grew up into a most beautiful girl, with wonderful golden hair. The witch called her Rapunzel, which is the witch word for lettuce. Soon she grew so very beautiful that the witch was sure someone would steal her and run away with her.

She made up her mind to build a tall tower, and lock the maiden up in it. So she built one, with a tiny window right at the top. There was no door, and no stairway, so the girl could not get out, and no one could get in. She was kept quite safe there.

Every evening the witch came to see how Rapunzel was getting on. She could not get in to her except in one way, and that was a most curious one.

She stood beneath Rapunzel's window and called up to her. When Rapunzel leant out, the witch said:

'Rapunzel, Rapunzel, let down your hair,
  That I may climb without a stair!'

Then Rapunzel let down her lovely hair as golden as corn in the sunshine. It was in two plaits, and was so long that it reached right from the window to the ground.

The witch climbed up the plaits every day, and so entered the tower to talk to Rapunzel and give her food.

Now one day a prince came riding through the forest, and saw the strange little tower. He rode near and was surprised to hear someone singing. He rode round the tower, trying to find the door, and was astonished to find none at all. He did not see how there could be anyone singing in the tower if there was no way to get in. He listened. It was true – there really was someone singing, and singing with a very sweet voice too.

The prince rode away very puzzled. He determined

to go the next day, and hear the voice again, and perhaps catch a glimpse of the singer.

So the next day he rode that way. He was nearly there, when he saw an old witch hobbling through the forest not very far away, and he followed her.

Perhaps she has something to do with that strange tower, he thought.

He saw her stand at the bottom of the tower and cry out:

> 'Rapunzel, Rapunzel, let down your hair,
> That I may climb without a stair.'

To the prince's great astonishment he saw two long golden plaits let down, and the witch climbed up them.

'So *that's* why there's no door!' said the prince. 'Now I know the way in!'

Early next morning he went to the tower again, and stood at the bottom.

'Rapunzel, Rapunzel, let down your hair,
That I may climb without a stair,'

called the prince.

At once two long plaits came tumbling down to him, smelling sweet as flowers, and feeling as soft as silk. The prince took hold of them and at once climbed up to the window and jumped into the room.

Rapunzel was frightened to see anyone who was not the witch, for she had never seen anyone else since she was a baby. She crouched back into the tower, and looked at the prince in terror.

He thought he had never in his life seen anyone so beautiful. He spoke kindly to her and told her he would not harm her, because he loved her. Rapunzel soon smiled at him, and was very happy and excited. She was sorry when he had to go and made him promise to return the next day.

Day after day he came, and little by little he told her of the world and all that people did. She found it as good as a story, for the witch had never told her anything. The prince brought her silken threads every day, and told her to weave them into a rope, so that when it was long enough she could climb down it, and run away with him. Rapunzel worked at it when the prince was not there and sang merrily.

The witch knew nothing about the prince's visits, for she felt quite sure that no one knew of the tower, and even if they did she did not think anyone could possibly enter it. She would never have known anything at all if Rapunzel had not been careless one evening. As she was pulling the witch up by her golden plaits, she said, 'Old witch, I wonder why you are so much heavier than the prince who visits me?'

The witch was amazed and angry to find that someone had found Rapunzel. She jumped in at the window, and shook her fist at the girl.

'How dare you let anyone in here?' she cried, and in a rage she cut off Rapunzel's golden plaits, so that no one should ever climb up them again. She bade

Rapunzel go to sleep, for she meant to wait for the prince in the tower, and punish him when he came.

The witch fell asleep before Rapunzel did, and then the unhappy girl remembered the silken rope she had been making. Quietly she tied it to a nail and slipped it out of the window. Then she climbed out of the window herself, and slid down the rope.

'Now I am free,' she said, 'and I will go and find the prince and warn him.'

But Rapunzel did not know the way and soon she was quite lost. She sat down in the forest, and began to weep for fear of what would happen to the prince.

That night the prince went as usual to the tower, and called softly up:

'Rapunzel, Rapunzel, let down your hair,
    That I may climb without a stair!'

The witch at once let down Rapunzel's two plaits that she had cut off, and the prince climbed quickly up to the window. He was horrified to find the witch looking at him with angry green eyes, instead of his own Rapunzel.

'Aha! The bird has flown, you see!' snarled the witch. 'I will catch *this* bird instead though, and keep him here!'

She made a snatch at the prince, but he managed to turn quickly. Then alas! He lost his hold on the windowsill and fell downwards to the ground. He did not strike the ground, but fell into a thorn bush. But, although his life was saved, his eyes were scratched and blinded by the thorns.

Lonely and miserable, he groped his way into the forest, trying to find his way out. But he could not see, and soon he was lost. Then suddenly he heard a sweet song in the distance.

'Surely that is Rapunzel's voice!' he said, and went towards the sound as quickly as he could. Sure enough it was the maiden sitting on a mossy bank, shorn of her beautiful locks. When she saw the poor blinded prince, she ran to him in sorrow, and put her arms round his neck. Two big tears fell from her eyes on to his ... and lo and behold! His scratches were all healed, and he could see as well as ever. He took Rapunzel safely out of the forest, and made his way back to the palace.

There they were married, and soon forgot about the old witch and lived happily ever after.

The Princess and the Red Goblin

The Princess and the Red Goblin

BOBADIL, A pixie dressed as a wizard, was travelling with his faithful little bunny. One day, as he was passing through a wood, he thought he heard a sobbing and a crying. He stopped and listened. Yes, it was quite true.

He went in the direction of the sound and came to a tall tower, in the top of which was a fairy princess, leaning out of a window, sobbing bitterly. Her tears fell on to the ground below like rain.

'What is the matter?' asked Bobadil.

'Oh, go away,' said the princess. 'You will get caught by the Red Goblin if you don't.'

'I will risk that,' said Bobadil. 'Tell me why you are crying.'

'I am crying because I am the goblin's prisoner,' said the princess, 'and he wants to marry me. I love a noble prince, who comes every day to try to rescue me, but in vain. See, here he comes.'

Bobadil heard footsteps and saw a handsome prince nearby. The princess called out to him and begged him to tell Bobadil to run while there was time.

'Yes, go quickly,' said the prince sadly. 'I am in the goblin's power too. He told me that if I could ask him to do anything he was not able to do he would set my princess free. He gave me twelve days to do this, and alas! Everything that I have so far asked him he has done. Today is my last chance, and I can think of nothing.'

'What have you asked him to do?' asked Bobadil.

'Well, I have asked him to build me a castle in a single night,' said the prince. 'I have asked him to bring me the most valuable necklace in the world.

I have even asked him to give me a thousand soldiers of my own.'

'Did he do all this?' asked Bobadil in astonishment.

'Oh yes,' said the prince with a sigh. 'The castle is quite near here, and the thousand soldiers are guarding it for me. I gave the necklace to my sweet little princess, but of what use are castles and soldiers to me, or necklaces to her, if I am not to marry her? We shall both be miserable all our lives long.'

'What else did you ask for?' said Bobadil.

'I asked for a hundred bags of gold,' said the prince, 'and the most beautiful and fastest horse in the world. I begged him to get me a cloak that would make me invisible when I put it on, and a sword that would cut through anything. I made him get me wings that I could fasten to my ankles and fly as fast as a swallow. All of these he got me and other things besides.'

'Oho,' said Bobadil. 'If you will trust yourselves to me, I think I can rescue you both from the Red Goblin without much difficulty.'

'Oh, wonderful wizard!' cried the prince gratefully. 'If you can only do that I will give you the hundred bags of gold.'

A hundred bags of gold! thought Bobadil. *Why, that would certainly make my fortune.*

'The Red Goblin lives in a great cave in the heart of the wood,' said the prince. 'I have got to go to him in ten minutes to ask him the twelfth thing. If he can do it, he will straight away come and marry the princess, and I shall be killed. How are you going to rescue us, wizard?'

'Change clothes with me quickly,' said Bobadil. 'I am going in your place, and if I don't manage to ask the goblin something he won't like I'll never try anything again.'

The prince quickly changed clothes with Bobadil. He put on the cloak and tall hat, while Bobadil put on the prince's feathered hat and smart tunic. When he was ready he turned to the prince.

'Follow me closely,' he said, 'and see what happens.'

The prince did as he was told, and together the two made their way into the wood. They came at last to a deep cave guarded at the entrance by two fierce cats. Bobadil's bunny was frightened when he saw them and crouched down behind some bushes, while his master entered the cave, leaving the prince outside.

Bobadil walked boldly into the cave, looking for the goblin. He came at last to a great hall, lit by a single star-shaped lamp in the middle. At the end of the hall sat the Red Goblin, a most unpleasant-looking creature.

'So you've come to make your last request,' said the goblin. 'Well, can you ask me anything that I shall not do?'

'Yes,' answered Bobadil. 'I will ask you to do something that you will not do.'

'What is that?' grinned the goblin unbelievingly.

'This is my twelfth request,' said Bobadil. 'Can you go right away from here and never come back again?'

The goblin sat upright at once when he heard what

Bobadil said. For some time he said never a word. Then he frowned and began to bite his stumpy nails.

'Ho, ho,' said Bobadil. 'That is something you cannot do, Red Goblin...and remember what you said would happen if you didn't do what was asked. You promised you would leave the princess to me, and let me take her away.'

The Red Goblin thought that the *prince* was speaking to him. He had no idea that it was Bobadil.

'I will go away on one condition,' he said, grinning wickedly. 'If you promise not to marry the princess yourself I will never bother you again.'

Bobadil smiled to himself when he heard this. *He* didn't want to marry the princess, so he could safely promise.

'Very well, I promise,' he said, sighing deeply to make the goblin think that he was grieved about it. 'All I want is that the dear princess shall be freed from the tower.'

'Free her then!' suddenly shouted the goblin

angrily. 'I am going right away now, but you will find it very difficult to get your precious princess free, I promise you! And if you do, you can't marry her, for you have vowed not to!'

With that he gave a yell, jumped straight up into the air and vanished. Bobadil couldn't see where he went, and stood staring in amazement. Then he hurried out to tell the prince what had happened.

But he found his way barred by the two fierce cats! They had let him in without so much as stirring a whisker, but they didn't mean to let him out again. They snarled at him, and showed their sharp white teeth, stretching out their claws in a most frightening way.

Oh, dear! thought Bobadil. *Now what am I to do? I daren't call the prince, or they may jump out at him and kill him. I wonder where my bunny is. Perhaps he could help me.*

The bunny wasn't very far away. He was still under his bush, watching the cave with wide-open brown eyes. When he saw the cats get up and snarl he guessed that his master was somewhere near, and he called out to warn him.

'Master Wizard!' he cried. 'Be careful, the cats are waiting for you.'

'I know,' said Bobadil. 'I can't think how to get past them.'

'*I'll* help you!' cried the brave little bunny. He suddenly ran out from his bush, and darted just by the two surprised cats. They stood and stared at him, and then, as he came by them again, they both made a dash and tried to spring on him. He was too quick, though, and tore off through the wood. Both cats forgot all about guarding the cave entrance, and went tearing after him.

That was Bobadil's chance! He ran out of the cave quickly, and ran to where the prince was anxiously waiting for him. He hurriedly told him all that had happened, and then looked and listened for the brave rabbit to come back to him. But he didn't come, and Bobadil felt very heavy of heart when he thought that perhaps the bunny had been caught by the two fierce cats.

'We cannot wait here any longer,' he said. 'We must go and rescue the princess at once. Change clothes with me again, prince, and go to the tower.'

Quickly the two put on their own clothes once more, and then made their way to the tower. But what a sight met their eyes there!

The tower had been changed, and was three times as high as before, so that the princess leaning out of the window at the top looked like a speck. She was so far away that they could not hear her voice.

Running round and round the tower was a spiral staircase, and on each step stood a goblin, just like the Red Goblin, but smaller. They carried sharp swords in their hands, and the prince was astonished when he saw them.

'Alas! Alas!' he said. 'This is the revenge of the goblin. He has had to go away and leave the princess, but he has put her in the hands of a hundred or more wicked goblins. Look at them, all standing there. I shall never be able to get past them all!'

'Yes, you will,' said Bobadil. 'Put your invisible cloak tightly round you, prince, then they won't see you. You can slip up all the stairs without any of them knowing!'

The prince was full of hope again, and pulled his cloak so tightly round him that not a bit of him was to be seen, and Bobadil only knew where he was by his voice.

'I'm going,' he said. 'I'll be back soon, Bobadil.'

Off he went, and slipped past all the watchful goblins unseen. They heard the patter of his feet, and stared in surprise, but as they could see no one they did nothing.

Up and up went the prince, up and up, until he came to the top of the tower. Here he found a door, strong and big, closed with a great bar of iron. The prince was in despair, for he tried to move it and could not. But he remembered his sword, and, taking it up, he hit the door a mighty blow with it. The blade cut through it as easily as a knife cuts cheese, and in one bound the prince was through it, and saw the frightened princess.

'It's your prince!' he cried, catching her up. 'Don't be frightened. I am going to take you away!'

She could not see him, but she knew his voice, and clung to him as he picked her up. At the same moment in came all the goblins, having heard the smashing of the door. They could not see the prince, but when they saw the princess swung off her feet they knew that a rescuer was there, and ran towards him, waving their swords.

The prince saw that he could not escape by the stairs, so he jumped on to the windowsill, holding the princess tightly, and then leapt into the air.

His ankle wings took him safely through the air, and the furious goblins watched the queer sight of the princess sailing off through the sky, seemingly by herself. Down the stairs they rushed, but they could do nothing.

Bobadil was at the bottom of the stairs looking up at the princess in great astonishment, having quite forgotten that the prince was wearing magic wings. There the goblins found him, and at once took him prisoner.

'Hands off me!' said Bobadil. 'I am a wizard, and it was all through me that the prince was able to rescue his princess and marry her.'

'*Marry* her!' shouted the goblins. 'But he promised not to.'

'Oh, no, he didn't,' grinned Bobadil. '*I* promised not to marry her, which is a very different thing, isn't it? It was I who was in the prince's clothes when the twelfth wish was asked.'

Well, the goblins were so astonished when they heard this that they decided to go away and tell their master about it.

'Take him into the very heart of the wood,' said one. 'Leave him there, for he can never find his way out by himself, and we shall easily find him again when we come back.'

So Bobadil was taken to the very middle of the wood, and left there in the deep shadow of the great trees. He was rather frightened, for he felt quite sure that he never *would* find his way out, and he couldn't quite think what to do.

'If only I were a *real* wizard, instead of just a pretend one,' he groaned. 'I could get out of here as easily as anything. I'm a wizard who isn't a wizard, and now I'm in a regular fix.'

Just at that moment he heard a scurry of little feet, and saw to his great delight his bunny coming scampering towards him.

'The cats got me into a hollow tree!' he panted, 'and it was ever such a long while till they went back to the cave again. Jump on my back, Master Wizard, and I will take you to the prince's castle.'

Bobadil gladly jumped on the rabbit's soft back, and off they went through the dark wood, till at last they came to a grand castle, guarded by a thousand fine soldiers.

The prince came running down the steps when he saw the wizard and the rabbit, and all the soldiers cheered.

'You're just in time for the wedding,' cried the prince. 'Come along quickly, for I have a hundred bags of gold to give you.'

Bobadil stayed for the wedding, and a very grand affair it was. Then he went on his way again, with a hundred soldiers in front of him, all carrying his bags of gold. He was very happy when he thought what a fine time he would have when he got home again, and what a grand party he would give to all his friends.

And so he did, but it wasn't very long before he was off on his adventures again, as you will hear another day!

The Tooth Under
the Pillow

The Tooth Under
the Pillow

ANNE WAS feeling rather excited. One of her first
teeth had come out that morning, and Mother had
said something surprising.

'We'll put it under your pillow tonight, Anne,'
she said.

'Why?' asked Anne.

'Because the fairies like the little first teeth of
children,' said Mother. 'Maybe one will come tonight
and take your tooth – and perhaps leave you a little
silver sixpence for it!'

That seemed very surprising to Anne. She thought
about it all day long – and she made up her mind that

she would keep awake that night so that she might see the fairy if one came!

Well, at night Anne put the tiny white tooth under her pillow and then she waited and waited for the fairy to come. But no fairy came.

I shall soon be asleep! thought Anne, yawning. *I wish I could think of some idea that would wake me up as soon as the fairy took the tooth!*

She did think of an idea! She got out of bed and went to Mother's workbox. She took out a reel of white cotton and broke off a piece of the thread. She tied it carefully around the little tooth and put it back under her pillow – and she tied the other end of the cotton to her own little finger!

Now! thought Anne, *if the fairy comes and takes the tooth – the thread will pull at my finger – and I shall wake up!*

She fell asleep. She dreamt of all kinds of things – and then suddenly she felt something tugging at her little finger! She woke up at once, and remembered the tooth under the pillow. The fairy must be there, fetching it.

The moonlight streamed into the room, and Anne could quite well see everything. By her bed stood a tiny creature, hardly bigger than Anne's biggest doll! She had a mop of bright shiny hair, little pointed ears that stuck up through it, and a pair of silvery wings that grew out from the back of her. There wasn't any doubt at all that it was a fairy.

Anne put out her hand and caught hold of her! She could hold her as easily as a doll. The fairy gave a squeal of surprise and began to wriggle hard. But Anne wouldn't let her go. She lifted her up on to the bed and took a good look at her.

'What a dear little thing you are!' she said. 'I did so want to see you. Have you come for my tooth?'

'Yes,' said the fairy. 'But it was on a bit of cotton. Why did you tie it to your finger?'

'Because I wanted to wake up when you came, and have a look at you,' said Anne. 'Why do you want my little tooth?'

'Well, it's made of bone,' said the fairy, 'which is nice to carve. I take children's little teeth to Mr Snoodle, and he carves them into tiny toys for fairy children.'

'Oh, how lovely!' said Anne. 'What tiny toys they must be! I would so like to see them.'

'You can't,' said the fairy. 'Mr Snoodle never lets any but fairy children have them.'

'Well, after all, it's *my* tooth!' Anne said. 'I don't think I shall let you go until you promise to bring me back the toy that my little tooth is carved into.'

'Oh, do let me go,' begged the tiny creature in alarm. 'I have to be back home before dawn. Everyone will be worried if I don't get back then.'

'Well, will you promise to bring me the toy that my tooth makes?' asked Anne. 'You needn't leave me the sixpence. I don't want that. I'd rather have my tooth back again, and see what Mr Snoodle has made of it!'

'I can't promise that,' said the fairy, beginning to wriggle again. 'Don't be unkind, little girl. Let me go. Mr Snoodle badly needs a few teeth just now. He hasn't had any for a long time.'

'Well, listen,' said Anne, 'I have two more teeth that are loose. I promise you that you shall have them for Mr Snoodle when they come out. I'll put them under my pillow. *Now* will you say that I can have this tooth when it's made into a toy?'

'Oh, well, if you really do promise to let me have two more teeth soon, I'll see what I can do about it,' said the fairy. 'Now please let me go!'

Anne let her go. The tiny thing spread her wings and fluttered down from the bed. She carried the little tooth with her on its thread. She flew out of the top of the window into the moonlight and was gone.

Anne felt very excited the next morning. She told her mother all about the fairy. Mother laughed and shook her head. 'You dreamt it, darling,' she said.

'Well, Mother, there's no sixpence under my pillow

this morning,' said Anne, 'so I'm sure I *did* catch the fairy and give her my tooth! Oh, won't it be fun if she comes back again with a tiny toy!'

Anne looked under her pillow every morning to see if a little ivory toy was there, but it wasn't. Then one evening another of her front teeth came out. *I'll put it under my pillow, and maybe the fairy will come back again*, thought Anne. *I'll tie it to my finger by a thread again. Then I shall wake.*

But, you know, she didn't wake! The fairy came – but this time she had a small pair of scissors with her, and she snipped the thread, so that she could take the tooth without waking Anne! When the little girl found that her tooth was gone, and that she still had a piece of cotton tied round her finger she guessed what had happened!

She hunted carefully under the pillow and in the bed – and she found the tiniest little toy imaginable. You would love it. It was a very, very small engine, carved out of her old tooth – so small that it could really hardly be seen! It had a tiny funnel, and it even had two very, very tiny lamps in front, carved out of it.

'Oh – it's simply beautiful!' cried Anne. 'Oh, I'll be afraid of losing it! Mother, Mother, look! What shall I do with this beautiful little fairy toy? I mustn't lose it. It's the most precious thing I have!'

'We will put it on to your bracelet,' said Mother. 'You shall wear it as a lucky charm. I'll do it for you now. What a lovely little thing it is!'

So Anne wears her engine tooth on her bracelet, and how all the children love to see it. Isn't she lucky?

She says I am to tell you that it really is a good idea to tie a bit of cotton to a tooth under the pillow – just in *case* you catch a fairy that way, as she did. It's worth trying, isn't it?

Beauty and the Beast

Beauty and the Beast

THERE WAS once a rich man who suddenly lost all his money. He took his lovely little daughter, Beauty, to live in a cottage in the country, where she had to do all the work herself.

But Beauty didn't mind a bit. She loved the sun and the flowers, and was as happy as the day is long, cooking and washing and sewing.

One day her father told her he must go on a journey and would perhaps not be back that night.

'What shall I bring you home for a present?' he asked.

'I would love a white rose!' said Beauty. 'We have

no white ones in our cottage garden.'

Off her father went, promising to bring her a beautiful white rose.

He rode to a far-away town, and soon did all that he had set out to do. He thought perhaps he would be able to get home before night, so he hurriedly mounted his horse, and set off.

But, alas, before he had gone very far, a storm came and he lost his way. When night came he found himself in a wood, but, try as he might, he could find no way out of it.

Suddenly he spied a light, far away in the distance. He rode towards it, thinking to find a woodman's cottage.

But, to his great astonishment, he found that he had come to a huge palace, with gates that stood wide open. He rode through them, up a long drive, and arrived at the palace door.

'Why, this is open too!' cried the man in surprise. 'And there's no one to be seen! Well, well, well!

I'll just walk in and see who I can find!'

He left his horse at the door and walked in. No one was about. The man went into the first room he saw, and found there a great blazing fire, and a table set with a lovely hot meal.

'Good gracious!' said the man, more and more surprised. 'This is just what I want. It's too late for me to get home tonight, so I'll go and stable my horse, and then come back and dry myself by this fire!'

He took his horse to the stable, and then came back to the warm room. He called and shouted and shouted and called, but no one came.

'Well, this meal is getting cold, for want of being eaten,' said the man, and straight away sat down and ate it.

After that he felt very sleepy, and wondered if there were any beds to be found. He went into the next room, and to his delight found a bed there all ready to be slept in. He undressed and jumped in.

In the morning he found that his own muddy suit

was gone, and a lovely one of silver put in its place.

'Well, what next?' cried the man as he jumped out of bed and dressed himself in silver cloth from top to toe.

Breakfast was all ready for him in the next room, and he ate a good meal. Then he called out thank you, and went to find his horse.

On his way to the stable he went through a lovely rose garden, and suddenly saw a beautiful bush of white roses.

'Dear me!' he said, stopping. 'I didn't get Beauty her white rose. I'll pick her one of these, and take it to her!'

He took hold of a beautiful bud and picked it. Then he jumped in fright and let it drop, for he heard a most terrible noise just behind him. He turned round, and saw a huge and ugly beast on the path, glaring at him.

'So this is the way you repay me for your fine meals, bed and clothes!' thundered the Beast. 'You steal my lovely white roses! You shall *die*!'

The poor man trembled and knelt down on the grass.

'Spare me, spare me!' he begged. 'I meant no harm!'

'I will spare you only if you bring me another life instead of your own,' said the Beast. 'If you will bring me whatever meets you first when you get home, I will spare your life!'

The man got up gladly and promised. He thought that one of his dogs would meet him first, and he hoped it would not be his favourite one. He ran to get his horse, mounted it, and set off home.

As he got near he looked out for his dogs. But alas, he saw none of them running to meet him, but instead his lovely daughter, Beauty!

'Welcome home, Father!' she cried. Then she stopped in distress for he looked so sad and troubled. 'What's the matter?' she asked. 'Are you ill?'

'Not ill, but terribly unhappy!' said her father, and he told her all that had happened.

'I promised to take to the Beast the first thing that met me when I got home!' he groaned. 'And *you* are that first thing, Beauty darling. But I shall not take you, of course. I shall go back myself.'

'No, take me, Father,' said Beauty bravely. 'You made the Beast a promise, and you must keep it. Perhaps he will not kill me.'

She begged so very hard that at last her father took her to the Beast's palace. In the room where he had had supper and breakfast before, was laid a delicious meal for two. The man told his daughter to sit down, and together they tried to eat, but both were so frightened and sad they could hardly touch anything.

Suddenly they heard a terrible noise at the door, and in walked the great, ugly Beast. Poor Beauty hid her face in her hands in fright.

'Do you bring this young girl in exchange for your life?' asked the Beast.

'She was the first thing that met me!' stammered the man. 'I have kept my promise to you, but I beg you to spare her, and kill me instead!'

'Don't be afraid,' said the Beast. 'I shall not kill her, nor you. I will take great care of her, and she shall have everything she wants. Bid her goodbye.'

The poor man kissed his sobbing daughter and left her. The Beast took her to a room, and told her it was hers.

Beauty could hardly see it for tears. But when she dried her eyes, she found herself in the most beautiful room she had ever seen. Pictures, flowers, rugs, books, everything she could possibly want was there.

There was a lovely mirror too, and under it was written a verse in gold letters. Beauty read it out loud.

'Little Beauty, dry your eyes,
Needless are those tears and sighs;
Gazing in this looking-glass
What you wish shall come to pass.'

That made Beauty feel happier, for she thought that if

she felt *too* sad she could just look into the glass and wish herself at home.

Day after day passed and Beauty lived in the Beast's palace. If she had not missed her father, she would have been very happy, for the palace and the gardens were beautiful, and she had everything she could possibly want.

Every evening the Beast came to see her eat her supper. Beauty was very much afraid of him at first, but soon she grew used to him, for he was very gentle and kind, and never frightened her in any way.

'Beauty, do you think I am very ugly?' the Beast asked one night.

'Yes, I do,' said Beauty sadly. 'But you are very kind!'

'Do you think I am very stupid?' asked the Beast.

'Oh, no,' said Beauty. 'You are a dear, gentle Beast.'

'Beauty, could you ever love me?' asked the Beast.

'I think I love you now,' said Beauty, 'because you are so kind to me.'

'Oh then do, *do* marry me!' begged the Beast.

'No, no!' said Beauty, covering her face, and thinking she could never marry such an ugly creature however kind and gentle he was.

The Beast went out of the room looking very sad and unhappy, and said no more to her.

Next day Beauty suddenly thought she would like to know how her father was. So she looked into the magic mirror in her room and wished that she might see there what he was doing.

To her great dismay she saw in the mirror a picture of her father lying ill in bed with no one to look after him. She cried all day, and when the Beast came that evening, he saw how red her eyes were.

'Why, Beauty,' he said. 'What have you been crying for? Aren't you happy?'

'Oh, yes, Beast, I am usually,' said Beauty, 'but today I looked into my magic mirror and saw my father lying ill and all alone. Please, Beast, dear, kind Beast, let me go home and look after my father.'

'I shall be heartbroken if you leave me, Beauty,' said the Beast, looking as if he too might cry at any moment. 'But I can't bear to see you looking so unhappy, so you may go to your father and make him better.'

'Oh, thank you, thank you!' cried Beauty in delight. 'When can I go?'

'Tomorrow,' said the Beast sadly. 'Look into your magic mirror tonight, Beauty, just before you get into bed, and wish to be home. Then in the morning you will wake up in your father's cottage.'

The Beast looked so miserable at the thought of losing her that Beauty felt very sorry for him.

'Don't look so sad,' she begged him. 'I will come back to you in a week.'

'Alas, Beauty, I fear you will never come back once I let you go!' said the Beast, sighing. 'But see – here is a magic ring. If you want to come back, lay it on your table at home before you go to bed, and wish to be here again. Then the next morning you will wake up in my palace.'

Beauty took the ring, and wished him goodbye. He went out sadly, and left Beauty alone. Before she went to sleep she looked in the magic mirror, and wished her wish, and jumped into bed.

Imagine how delighted she was the next morning to wake up in her own little bed in her father's cottage. She jumped out and ran straight into her father's room.

'Father!' she cried. 'I have come back to look after you.'

Her father was so surprised and overjoyed to see her that he couldn't say a word to greet her. He just looked at her and smiled happily.

Beauty began to nurse him and to give him all the good food he needed. She laughed and sang and danced, and soon her father began to laugh and sing too, and no longer needed to keep to his bed.

A whole week went by, and Beauty forgot to keep count of the days. Then another week went by, and still

Beauty forgot how quickly time went. She thought only of her father and of getting him well quickly.

Then one night she had a very *peculiar* dream. She dreamt she was back in the palace gardens again, and saw the big, ugly Beast lying on the grass beneath the bush of white roses she loved so much. He looked ill, and he was saying, sadly, 'Oh, Beauty, little Beauty, it is two weeks now that I have looked for you, and you have not come. My heart is broken, for I know I shall never see you again. I shall soon die for want of you!'

Beauty woke up with a jump, and began to think of the Beast, and how kind he had been to let her leave him and go home. Then she remembered that she had said she would go back to him in a week.

'And dear, dear me!' said Beauty in dismay. 'It must be quite two weeks since I have been home! Whatever must the poor Beast be thinking! I will go back to him at once.'

She jumped out of bed, and put her magic ring on

the table. She wished to be back in the palace again, jumped into bed once more and fell asleep.

Next morning, she awoke in her beautiful little bed at the palace. She wondered if the Beast were anywhere about, but as he never came to visit her until evening, she had to wait all day.

When she sat down to her supper, she listened for the Beast's footsteps outside the door. But none came.

She waited a little while, and then began her supper. No Beast came. Beauty couldn't make it out.

She finished her supper, and then sat quite still listening. But however much she listened, she could hear nothing at all – no footsteps, no knock at the door and no deep voice.

'Wherever can he be?' wondered Beauty miserably. 'He *always* comes to talk to me at supper time. Is he cross with me?'

She sat for another hour waiting. Then a thought came into her mind. She would go and find him!

Up she jumped and ran out of the room. Up and

down the castle she hunted, but nowhere could she find the Beast.

'He's nowhere indoors!' said Beauty. Then she stopped and thought. 'Oh, dear, oh, dear!' she cried. 'Perhaps my dream was true, and the poor Beast is lying underneath my white rose bush!'

Off she ran into the moonlit garden – and there on the grass lay the poor, ugly Beast, as if he were dead.

'Beast! Beast!' cried Beauty in fright. 'Open your eyes and look at me! Here is Beauty come back to you! Open your eyes, dear Beast!'

To Beauty's great delight the Beast opened his great brown eyes. He smiled with joy when he saw Beauty.

'My darling Beauty!' he whispered gladly. 'So you have come back to me! I thought you had gone for ever and I could not live without you. I shall die in happiness now that I know you have come back!'

'You mustn't die, you mustn't die!' cried Beauty, putting her arms round his neck. 'I love you, Beast, and I will marry you, truly I will. You are so kind and gentle!'

She hid her face in her hands and began to cry, for she was very unhappy and grieved to find her Beast so ill. When she looked up again to comfort him, he was gone!

Beauty started in astonishment, for just a moment before the Beast had lain on the ground.

Then she heard a deep, gentle voice behind her.

'Thank you, Beauty darling, for setting me free,' said the voice.

Beauty jumped, and looked to see who had spoken – and to her great astonishment she found standing by her a tall, handsome prince!

'Who are you?' she cried. 'And what do you mean? What have you done with my dear Beast? Where is he gone?'

'Hush, Beauty,' said the prince, taking her hands in his, and raising her from the ground. 'Don't be frightened. *I* was the Beast. Long ago a wicked witch enchanted me, and turned me into the ugly Beast you knew. I had to remain ugly and stupid until a beautiful lady came and said she would marry me! And you, Beauty dear, are the beautiful lady!'

Beauty looked at him in surprise and delight. So this was the ugly Beast – this handsome, smiling young prince! How delighted she was!

'Oh please let my father know!' she begged.

And in five minutes a good fairy brought her father to her, and Beauty proudly showed him what had happened to the ugly Beast.

Then the wedding bells rang out and Beauty and her prince were married. They lived happily in the lovely palace, and on every birthday that Beauty had, the prince picked a lovely bunch of white roses and put them on her plate, and wrote by them:

'To darling Beauty, from the Beast.'

Old Mother Wrinkle

Old Mother Wrinkle

OLD MOTHER Wrinkle was a strange old dame. She lived in an oak tree, which had a small door so closely fitted into its trunk that nobody but Dame Wrinkle could open it. It was opened many times a day by the old dame, for always there seemed to be somebody knocking at her door.

The little folk came to ask her to take away their wrinkles. Fairies never get old as we do – but sometimes, if they are worried about anything, they frown or sulk, and then lines and wrinkles grow in their faces. Frown at yourself in the glass and see the ugly wrinkle you get.

Mother Wrinkle could always take away any wrinkle, no matter how deep it was. She would take a fairy into her round tree room, sit her down in a chair and look at her closely.

'Ho!' she might say. 'You've been feeling cross this week. There's a very nasty wrinkle right in the middle of your forehead. Sit still, please!'

Then she would rub a curious-smelling ointment on the fairy's forehead to loosen the wrinkle. Then she took up a very fine knife and carefully scraped the wrinkle off. She powdered the fairy's forehead and told her to go.

'But don't you frown any more,' she would call after her. 'It's a pity to spoil your pretty face.'

Now Mother Wrinkle had taken wrinkles away for two hundred years, and the inside of her room was getting quite crowded with the wrinkles. She didn't like to throw them away, for she was a careful old dame. She packed them into boxes and piled them one on top of another.

But soon the boxes reached the top of her room – really, there must be a million wrinkles packed into them. What in the world could Mother Wrinkle do with them?

Now the fairies did not pay her for taking away their wrinkles. Sometimes they brought her a little pot of honey, sometimes it was a new shawl made of dandelion fluff – but the old dame hardly ever had any money, and she needed some badly.

'I want a new table,' she said, looking at her old worn one. 'I would love a rocking chair to rock myself in when I'm tired. And how I would like a pair of soft slippers for my old feet!'

She told the sandy rabbit this one day when he came to bid her good morning. He nodded his long-eared head. 'Yes,' he said, 'you do want some new things, Mother Wrinkle. Well, why don't you sell those boxes of wrinkles and get a little money?'

'Sell the wrinkles!' cried the old dame. 'Why, I'd love to – but who would buy them? Nobody! If people want to get rid of wrinkles they certainly wouldn't pay money to get some. That's a silly idea, Sandy Rabbit.'

The rabbit lolloped off, thinking hard. He liked the old woman. She was always generous and kind. He wished he could help her. He talked to the pixies about it. He spoke to the frogs. He told the hedgehog. He spoke to the bluebell fairy – and, last of all, he met the little primrose fairy, and told her.

She listened carefully and then she thought hard. She had been very worried for the last fifty years because the primroses, which were her special care, had been dreadfully spoilt each spring by the rain. Whenever it rained, the wet clung to the leaves, ran down to the centre of the plant and spoilt the pretty yellow flowers. It was such a nuisance. She had been so worried about it that Mother Wrinkle had had to scrape away about twenty wrinkles from her pretty forehead.

But now she had an idea. Suppose she took the wrinkles that the old dame had got in her boxes!

Suppose she pressed them into the primrose leaves! Suppose she made them so wrinkled that when the rain came the wrinkles acted like little riverbeds and drained the water off at once, so that it didn't soak the leaves and spoil the flowers!

What a good idea that would be! thought the primrose fairy joyfully. *I'll try it.*

So she went to Mother Wrinkle and bought one box of wrinkles. She took them to her primrose dell and set to work. The primrose leaves, in those days, were as smooth and as thin as beech leaves – but when the fairy began to press the wrinkles into the leaves, what a difference it made!

One by one the leaves looked rough and wrinkled. In the middle of her work the rain came down, and to the fairy's great delight the wrinkles acted just as she had hoped – the rain ran into them and trickled to the ground in tiny rivulets!

'Good!' said the fairy in delight. 'Now listen, primrose plants! You must grow your leaves in a rosette and point them all outwards and downwards. Then, when the rain comes, your wrinkles will let it all run away on the outside – and your flowers will be kept dry and unspoilt.'

Little by little the fairy gave wrinkles to every primrose plant, and they grew well, till the woods were yellow with the flowers in spring. Mother Wrinkle was delighted to sell the old wrinkles. She bought herself a new table, a fine rocking-chair, and two pairs of soft slippers.

And now you must do something to find out if this strange little story is true. Hunt for the primrose plant – and look at the leaves! You will see the wrinkles there as sure as can be – delicate and fine – but quite enough to let the rain run away without spoiling the pale and lovely flowers.

The Four-Leaved
Clover

The Four-Leaved Clover

'LINDA!' CALLED Mother. 'It's time to go to your dancing lesson. Hurry up!'

Mother didn't need to tell Linda to make haste for her dancing lesson! It was the lesson Linda liked best of all, and she didn't mind a bit giving up Saturday morning for it. She was always ready at least ten minutes before the bus went.

She came running downstairs, dressed in her little white fluffy frock with her coat over it. She had her shoes in her bag.

'Here's the money for the bus,' said Mother, and gave it to her. 'Got your shoes – and a clean hanky?'

'Yes, of course!' said Linda. 'I'll go now, Mother. Hurray, it's dancing lesson today!'

Linda was a very good little dancer, very quick at learning all kinds of new steps.

'You're as light as a fairy!' the dancing mistress said to her that morning. 'I really feel that you must sometimes have wings, Linda, wings we can't see, the way you spring here and there, and come down without the slightest sound!'

Linda wished she *was* a fairy! How marvellous to have wings and fly! But she had never even seen a fairy, though she had hidden behind trees for hours and watched.

'Mother,' she said, one day, 'is there any way that people can have wishes that come true nowadays?'

'Well,' said Mother, 'there aren't any fairies about here to give you a wish and there are no wishing wands for sale, and certainly no wishing-caps. You'll just have to find a four-leaved clover!'

'A four-leaved clover!' said Linda. 'But a clover

is three-leaved, not four.'

'I know,' said Mother, 'but sometimes, just *some*times, you can find one with four leaves on the stem, instead of three. And that's supposed to have a little magic in it.'

'*Really?*' said Linda, excited. 'What kind of magic?'

'Well, a four-leaved clover is always lucky,' said Mother, 'and some of them are supposed to be magic enough to grant one wish – but only one. I've never found one – they're very rare.'

'I shall go and look in the clover patches on the lawn till I *do* find one!' said Linda. 'And I know what I shall wish if I do! I shall wish I was a fairy with wings, and could fly!'

'Oh dear,' said Mother. 'Don't wish that – I'd rather have you as you are, a dear little girl!'

'I suppose I couldn't be both,' said Linda. 'What a pity. But if I *do* find a four-leaved clover, I shall simply *have* to wish I could be a fairy with wings and fly, Mother. You don't know how badly I want to.'

Now, will you believe it, the third time that Linda went to hunt for a four-leaved clover on the lawn she found one! At first she couldn't believe it – but there it was! She picked it very carefully indeed and looked at it.

'You've got four leaves, not three,' she said, and her voice shook with excitement. 'You're magic! I'm going to wish my wish. Are you listening, clover?'

The clover shook in the breeze. Linda held it up and wished. 'I wish I could be a fairy with wings, and fly in the air!'

She waited. Would she turn into a fairy straight away, with wings on her back? Did they take time to grow? She wondered if she would feel them growing. How soon would she be able to fly?

Nothing happened. She put her hand round to her back to see if any wings were sprouting there. If they were she would have to go indoors and ask Mother to cut holes in her frock so that they could grow out.

But nothing was growing there. She couldn't even

feel any little bumps that would tell her that wings were coming. It was really very disappointing.

I must have found a four-leaved clover that isn't magic enough to grant me a wish, she thought. *Oh, dear – and I was so pleased to think I might really have my wish at last!*

'Mother,' said Linda, when she went indoors, 'I found a four-leaved clover – look! But it isn't magic. It's very disappointing.'

'Never mind, dear,' said Mother. 'Put it in between the pages of your favourite book. It will always be lucky, even if it doesn't grant a wish!'

It was Saturday afternoon and Linda had already had her dancing lesson that morning. It was three o'clock now – what should she do till teatime?

'Mother, I'll take Scamper for a walk,' she said. 'He's longing to go!'

So she set off with Scamper. She walked down the lane and came to the main road. She thought she would go into the town and look at the toy shops.

As she passed the town hall, she stopped to look at a big poster there.

GRAND SHOW TONIGHT, said the poster. PANTOMIME FOR THE CHILDREN.

Oh, dear – I wish I'd known, then perhaps Mother would have taken me, thought Linda. *Now I expect all the tickets will be gone.*

She went to ask. Yes, every single one had been sold. What a pity!

As she stood looking at the pictures in the porch of the town hall, two or three people came out from the hall itself.

'Well, the rehearsal went all right,' said one of them. 'But *what* are we going to do about that child who has been taken ill? Can we possibly replace her?'

'I shouldn't think so,' said another man. 'We *must* have someone who can dance. Pity – the show won't be quite so good with one dancer less.'

Someone else came out and joined them. It was Miss Clarissa, who taught Linda dancing. She caught sight of the little girl and smiled. Then she suddenly stopped as if a thought had struck her. She went quickly up to the three men.

'I've got an idea. Do you see that child over there? Well, I teach her dancing, and she's as light as a fairy! I believe she could easily take the place of the child who is ill!'

The three men looked at Linda, and she went very red. 'Would you like to be one of the fairies in the pantomime tonight?' asked Miss Clarissa. 'You know all the steps of the dance, and if any are different you can easily follow the others in front of you.'

'But – but – what would my mother say?' said Linda, amazed.

'Go and ask her,' said one of the men. 'Go along and ask her now! Take her, Miss Clarissa. If you think she's good enough, we'll have her. The dress will fit all right.'

'Come along, Linda,' said Miss Clarissa, and hurried her off. She talked to her as she went along.

'There's a most beautiful dress to wear, and you have a wand and a pair of wings! You'll be just like a fairy!'

Linda could hardly speak. 'Will I fly?' she said at last.

'Well, we shall put you on a wire with the other fairies,' said Miss Clarissa, 'and swing you to and fro across the stage, and up and down – and you must flap your lovely wings, of course!'

'Oh,' said Linda, and her eyes shone. *My wish is coming true!* she thought. *It is, it is! I wished to be a fairy, and have wings and fly – and it's all going to happen! Mother said she still wanted me to be her own little girl, even if I was a fairy – and I shall be! I shall be a fairy and fly just for tonight!*

Well, Mother was just as excited as Linda, of course. She nodded her head to all that Miss Clarissa said.

'I know it will please Linda,' she said. 'She will feel like a real fairy flying through the air like that. Why, Linda, your four-leaved clover was magic after all!'

That night Linda went to the pantomime, but she didn't sit in the seats in front to watch. She was behind with all the other players! There were about twenty small girls, who were to dance – but only four of them were to fly – and one of those four was Linda!

The fairy frock fitted her beautifully, and she trembled with joy when they put on her beautiful big silvery wings. 'Move your shoulders to and fro and the wings will flap,' said Miss Clarissa. Linda moved her shoulders – and sure enough the wings flapped as if they grew out of her back.

'Here is your wand,' said Miss Clarissa.

Linda took it. 'Is there any magic in it?' she asked.

'No,' said Miss Clarissa. 'Not as much as in your four-leaved clover anyway! I never heard of a little girl before who wished to be a fairy with wings and fly – and whose wish came true in such a wonderful way. Now let me just see you do your steps, Linda – I'm sure you will dance as lightly as anyone.'

'Is my mother watching – and Daddy?' asked

Linda. 'Have they got seats?'

'Yes, right in the very front,' said Miss Clarissa. 'You won't be frightened when you fly in the air, will you, Linda?'

'Of course not,' said Linda. 'It's what I'm looking forward to most of all!'

The time came for the fairies to go on the stage. They tripped on, waving their wands and began to dance. Linda danced best of all. She couldn't help it; she was so happy. She really was as light as a fairy, and soon everyone was watching the little girl with dark hair and dark eyes, dancing as if she was in a lovely dream.

Then came the part where four of the fairies were to fly! Linda and three others had strong wires fixed to them and, quite suddenly, they were lifted right off their feet into the air! Linda wasn't expecting it, and she gasped for joy. Her wings flapped gently, and she laughed in delight.

I'm flying, she thought. *I'm flying! So this is what flying is like – lovelier even than I thought! Oh, I'm glad my wish came true!*

The fairies were clapped and clapped. Then somebody called out. 'Where's the little dark fairy? She was the best of all – she's a *real* fairy!'

Miss Clarissa pushed Linda out on to the stage alone. She was bewildered. She didn't curtsey, because she didn't know why she had been pushed alone on to the stage. Then suddenly the wire pulled her up into the air once more, and she gave a scream of delight.

'I'm flying again!' she cried. 'I'm flying!'

Everyone laughed and clapped madly. Her mother almost cried with pride and delight as she watched Linda flying gracefully to and fro all by herself. Then the wire swung her down to the stage again, and she remembered to curtsey.

'Well done, Linda,' said Miss Clarissa, pleased, when Linda came running off, still flapping her wings. 'Come and see the stage manager – he's delighted.'

'Good girl!' said the big stage manager to Linda.

'Now, I want to give you a present for being such a good fairy. What would you like? Ask for any toy you want!'

Linda's eyes shone. 'I don't want a toy,' she said. 'But – oh – do you think I could *possibly* keep my fairy wings?'

'Of course,' said the big man. 'I suppose you think you'll go flying off every night on them? Well, happy journeys!'

Linda couldn't go to sleep that night. Her wings were on a chair beside her bed. She kept putting her hand out and touching them to make sure they were there.

My wish came true! she kept thinking. *I didn't think it would, but it did – in a really magic way! Oh, I'm glad I found that four-leaved clover. Perhaps one day I'll find another and wish that I can fly again.*

Perhaps she will. I hope *you* find a four-leaved clover, too. Take care of it if you do.

The Imp Without a Name

The Imp Without
a Name

THERE WAS once an imp whose name nobody knew. He was little and nimble, with green eyes like a cat, and a long tail that he wore tied round his waist.

He came to live in Hollyhock Town, though nobody wanted him to. Hollyhock Town was beautiful, and all the cottages were as bright and neat as a new pin. Hollyhocks grew there all the year round, and marigolds and poppies and sweet williams shone in every garden.

But not in the imp's garden. No – nothing grew there at all, except weeds. The imp was lazy. He wouldn't dig. He wouldn't sow seeds. He wouldn't hang his garden gate straight when it went crooked. He wouldn't get his window mended when he broke it. He wouldn't wash his curtains, so they got blacker and blacker, because the chimney smoked, and the imp was too lazy to sweep it.

The folk of Hollyhock Town wished they could make the imp leave, for his dirty, untidy house and garden spoilt their pretty town. It stood right in the middle and everyone could see it. If only it had been tucked away somewhere it wouldn't have been so bad!

'Let's go to the next council meeting in Fairyland and ask if we can send the imp away somewhere else,' said the old gnome, Snoozy.

'Yes, that's a good idea,' said Hallo the brownie, his sharp eyes twinkling. 'Four of us will go and say what a nuisance he is, and ask the council to write to him and make him leave our neat little village.'

So they went to the next council meeting and asked the chairman if they might do what they wanted.

THE IMP WITHOUT A NAME

'Certainly,' he said, taking up his pen. 'I will send him a notice myself. What is his name?'

'We don't know,' said Hallo the brownie. 'He has never told anyone, and we can't find out.'

'Oh, well,' said the chairman, putting down his pen, 'I can't write to someone who hasn't a name! You must find his name and I'll send the notice then.'

The four from Hollyhock Town went back home, wondering how they could find out the imp's name. If he wouldn't tell them, what were they to do? Nobody knew who he was or where he came from, or even if he had any friends. It was a puzzle.

'I know!' said Hallo, looking at the others with his bright eyes. 'I'll slip into his house, when he is out, and see if his name is in any of his books. People often have their names in their books, you know.'

'Yes, that's a good idea,' said Snoozy. 'But be sure not to get caught, Hallo. The imp knows a lot of magic – you might find yourself in a tight fix if he caught you.'

'I'll be careful,' said Hallo. So he watched and waited for the imp to go out. This was easy, because Hallo lived opposite to the imp. He thought he would do some gardening, and then, from his front garden, he could see when the imp went out.

I'll dig up my front bed and plant my mustard and cress there, thought Hallo to himself. *I shan't be wasting my time then.*

So he got a packet of mustard seeds and a packet of cress seeds, and went into his front garden. He began to dig – and he hadn't dug for more than ten minutes when he heard the door of the imp's house bang. He looked up. The imp was going down the road.

'Hi! Are you off to catch the bus?' asked Hallo at once.

'Yes,' said the imp. 'I'm going away for the day. See you later. Goodbye!'

Ha! thought Hallo, pleased. *That's very good. I can get into his house and look for his name as long as I like.*

He washed his hands, put away his spade, and then

ran across the road to the imp's dirty, untidy house. The front door was locked, so he went to the back. That was locked too. But there was a window open, and Hallo soon slipped inside.

Then he began to look round. There were a great many books there. He opened them, one after the other, hoping to see the imp's name written in them. But no – there didn't seem to be a name written anywhere at all. Hallo looked through at least fifty books, and then sighed. It was a tiring job looking for something he so badly wanted to find and couldn't.

Well, it was no good – there wasn't a name in any of the books. Perhaps the imp had his name marked on his clothes! Hallo went into the little bedroom and looked at the coats hanging up; no – not a single name was on those either!

Then he suddenly thought of the imp's desk. Perhaps his name would be on papers there. He went to the kitchen where he had seen a desk – but it was locked. Hallo was just turning away in despair when he caught sight of a letter that the imp had written to someone. And at the bottom he had signed his name. Yes – there it was, quite plain to see!

Hallo read it. 'Tom-Tit-Tot! Oh ho! So that's your name, little imp! Tom-Tit-Tot!'

'Yes,' said a voice suddenly. 'That's my name – you horrid little sneaking brownie! What do you mean by coming here when I'm out?'

Hallo looked up in fright. Goodness gracious, the imp had come back quietly, let himself in – and there he was standing by Hallo, a horrid look on his face.

'I came to look for your name, not to steal anything,' said Hallo. 'And I know it now – yes – Tom-Tit-Tot!'

The imp was angry. If people knew his name they would know who he was and the bad things he had done, and he might be turned out of Fairyland! He caught hold of Hallo and shook him.

'Well, it won't do you any good finding out my name,' he said. 'Because I shall send you away to the Land of Lost People, and you'll not come back!

Ho, ho! Tell my name in that land all you like – but you won't find anyone who wants to know it.'

Hallo was frightened. 'Let me go,' he begged. 'I won't tell your name to anyone if you'll only let me go. I'm sorry I came to find it.'

'No, I shan't let you go,' said the imp. 'You will ride on the white owl's back to the Lost Land tonight.'

'Can't I even go and plant my mustard and cress seeds?' wept Hallo. 'I only bought them today.'

'Well, you can plant them in *my* garden!' said the imp with a grin. 'I'd like some mustard-and-cress sandwiches! Go and plant them now – and, mind, if you so much as say a word to anyone passing by, I'll pull your nose till it's as long as a cucumber.'

Hallo went out into the garden. He was very frightened. Nobody came by at all, so he couldn't have said anything to anyone if he wanted to. As he dug up the ground, a sudden thought came to him.

He knew a way of telling the imp's name to everyone. Ah, he knew a fine way. He would plant the mustard and cress so that when they came up they would grow into the imp's name. Hallo often planted the seeds so that his own name, 'Hallo', grew up green and fresh. Aha! Although he would be sent far away to the Lost Land, and be one of the Lost People, the folk of Hollyhock Town would know the imp's name all the same when the mustard and cress grew up.

He quickly planted the seeds, and then went back into the imp's cottage. It grew dark. A loud screech was suddenly heard outside – the white owl had arrived. It did not hoot, but screeched in a most tiresome manner.

Hallo got on its back and flew off sadly to the Land of Lost People. The imp banged his door, made himself a cup of cocoa, and grinned from ear to ear. He had known quite well that Hallo meant to sneak into his house and find out his name – and he had only pretended to go off for the day. The imp was clever, and his green eyes shone like a cat's as he laughed to himself.

The summer went on. The seeds began to grow. But the folk in Hollyhock Town thought nothing of seeds growing – they only thought of Hallo – where could he have gone? They were dreadfully afraid that he had been caught by the imp and sent off somewhere, never to come back. But the imp shook his head and said nothing, no matter what they asked him.

Now one day, when the children of the town ran by the imp's untidy garden, one of them peeped over and saw his mustard and cress. 'Oh!' he said in surprise. 'It's growing into a name.'

But the children could not read the name, so they soon ran off. One of them told his mother and she ran to tell Snoozy, the old gnome. He listened in amazement, and then at once took up his hat and went to see.

He looked a long time at the garden where the mustard and cress were growing. 'The name is upside down from here,' he said. 'I must go in and see it the right way up.' So through the gate he went, and then he could read the name easily in the green mustard and cress. 'Tom-Tit-Tot!' he read. 'Tom-Tit-Tot! My goodness, is that the imp's name? Surely he wouldn't be so foolish as to grow it in mustard and cress for everyone to see. No – Hallo, the brownie, must have found it out, and managed to plant it in the garden before the imp sent him off somewhere.'

He hurried home and wrote to the council, telling them all he knew and all he feared. The very next day a grand gnome drove up in his carriage and knocked at Snoozy's door.

'Good morning,' he said. 'We got your letter. This is most important, Snoozy – for if that imp is really Tom-Tit-Tot, we have been looking for him for years. He stole a crown belonging to the queen, then escaped, and we haven't heard of him since. No wonder he would tell nobody his name. Where does he live?'

Snoozy took him to the imp's cottage. The imp was just going out to do his shopping. The grand gnome put his hand on his shoulder, and said sternly, 'Tom-Tit-Tot, come with me. You stole the queen's crown many years ago – but it is not too late for you to be punished for it.'

'That is not my name,' said the imp boldly.

'Then why do you grow it in mustard and cress in your garden?' said the great gnome sternly. The imp stared at the mustard and cress in horror. He hadn't even noticed that it grew his name. Hallo had been cleverer than he had thought him to be.

'Yes,' said the great gnome. 'There it is – Tom-Tit-Tot. And where is the brownie you caught and sent away, Tom-Tit-Tot?'

Then the imp, full of fear, told all he knew. He was taken away to be judged – and the white owl was sent to the Land of Lost People to bring back Hallo.

There was a great feast when Hallo came back. People crowded round him, and praised him for his cleverness in leaving behind the imp's name in mustard and cress – and what do you suppose the sandwiches were at the feast? Guess!

Yes – you are quite right – they were made of mustard and cress from Tom-Tit-Tot's untidy garden!

The Disappointed
Sprites

The Disappointed Sprites

ONCE UPON a time the little water sprites were very sad. They sat swinging in the rushes that grew by the side of the lake, and talked about their trouble.

'I don't think it's fair!' said Willow. 'Why shouldn't we be allowed to dance in the fairy ring too! I do think that the fairies are mean!'

'Is it *really* true that they said we weren't to dance with them any more?' asked Trickle.

'Yes, didn't you know?' said Splashabout. 'They sent us a letter this morning. Read it, Willow.'

Willow took a letter from her pocket and spread it out. 'This is what they say,' she began. '*Dear*

Water Sprites, please do not come and dance in our fairy ring any more. You spoil our dances. With love from the fairies.'

'Well! How very horrid of them!' cried Trickle. 'Why don't they want us any more? We behave quite nicely!'

'Let's go and ask them!' said Splashabout. 'And if we think their reason is fair, we won't make a fuss. But if it isn't, we'll go and complain to the queen.'

So the three little sprites set off over the grass to Pixie Town among the toadstools. Here were fairies and elves, pixies and brownies. They all stared at the three sprites as they came running up, and wondered what was the matter.

'What do you want?' they cried. 'Have you lost something?'

'No,' answered Willow, 'but we want to know why we aren't allowed to come and dance with you any more. What have we done to upset you?'

'Nothing,' said a fairy. 'It isn't really your fault.'

'Well, whose fault is it then?' asked Splashabout impatiently. 'We think it's very mean of you.'

The pixies and fairies looked at each other. Nobody wanted to explain. At last a brownie broke the silence.

'It's like this,' he said. 'You're always so *wet*, and when we dance with you we spoil our clothes.'

'And you make all the seats wet too, with your damp frocks,' said an elf.

'And I've got a dreadful cold through putting on one of your wet shawls by mistake. Atishoo! Atishoo!' said a pixie, and blew his nose loudly.

The sprites stared sadly at the fairies.

'But we can't *help* being wet,' said Trickle sorrowfully. 'We live in the water, you see. We're *always* wet and we never get colds.'

'That's because you're used to it,' said a fairy. 'We aren't, and we feel as if we're dancing with frogs when we dance with you.'

'We're awfully sorry about it, but you do spoil all our dances.'

The three water sprites looked at each other, and decided to be brave about it.

'We're sorry,' said Willow. 'We quite understand.'

'But it's dreadfully disappointing, because we do so like dancing,' said Trickle, nearly crying.

'And there's no place on the water where we can dance,' said Splashabout.

They said goodbye, and went sadly back to the lake. They told all the water sprites what they had heard, and everyone was very upset.

'That's the end of all our dancing,' said Ripple. 'And it's a great pity, for we are the lightest and daintiest of all fairy folk.'

'Well, we must just make the best of it,' said Willow. 'We'll go and watch next time the fairies have a dance, but we won't go near enough to wet them.'

So next time the elves and fairies held a dance in the fairy ring, the sprites crept up to watch them. They heard the music played by the grasshoppers and bees, and longed to join in the dance, but they had made up their minds to be good – and so they were.

Carefully they hid themselves in the long grass around the fairy ring and peeped out from behind the wild flowers to watch quietly.

Now, it happened that the fairy queen decided to go to the dance that night. She floated down, pale and beautiful in the moonlight, and took her place on the little silver throne that always stood waiting for her.

The fairies were delighted to see her, and made a great fuss of her, for she was very good to them.

'Go on with your dancing,' she said. 'I'd love to watch you.'

So they all danced and tripped, and pranced and skipped, as merry as could be, till suddenly the queen wondered where the water sprites were. They had never missed a dance before, and she couldn't think why they weren't there. She peeped all round the dancers, but not one sprite could she see.

And then she suddenly spied them peeping and peering behind the buttercups and daisies outside the fairy rings! She *was* astonished!

She clapped her hands and ordered the dance to stop for a minute. The music stopped and everyone turned to hear what Her Majesty had to say.

'Why do the water sprites peep and hide, instead of dancing?' she asked. 'Have they been naughty?'

'Oh, no, Your Majesty!' answered a pixie. 'They're not at all naughty. But we asked them not to come to our dances any more.'

'Why did you do that?' asked the queen in astonishment.

'Because they are always so dreadfully wet!' answered the pixie. 'They ruin our clothes and make us catch terrible colds.'

'But haven't they anywhere to dance now?' asked the queen.

'No, nowhere,' said the pixies sadly. 'They can't dance on the lake, you see, and we can't have them in our dancing rings any more.'

'Dear, dear!' said the queen. 'Whatever can

we do! Were the water sprites nice about it, or were they angry?'

'They were ever so nice,' said all the fairies at once.

'The promised not to come!' said a brownie.

'And they said they were sorry and quite understood!' called an elf.

The queen was pleased. She liked to hear of people taking a disappointment cheerfully. She waved her hand.

'Go on with your dancing,' she said, looking thoughtful.

The bees and grasshoppers began playing again, and the fairies took their partners and went merrily on with their dance.

They didn't see the queen slip away through the grass. She went very quietly, her crown gleaming like dewdrops in the bright moonlight.

She went to the lake. It lay very peaceful and still. All the sprites who usually played there were away watching the dance.

Big white and yellow water-lilies lay on the water. The queen called to them.

'Water-lilies,' she cried, 'where are your leaves?'

'Down in the water!' answered the water-lilies in voices like a hundred singing ripples.

'Listen!' said the queen. 'Raise them to the top of the lake, and let them spread themselves smooth and flat on the water.' The lilies all raised their leaves and did as they were told. Gradually the lake became spread with big flat leaves, shining in the moonlight.

'Thank you,' said the queen. 'You look beautiful now, water-lilies. Will you let the little water sprites dance on your leaves when the lake is calm?'

'Yes! Yes!' said the water-lilies softly. 'We love the water sprites; they look after our buds for us!'

Then the queen called the green frogs to her, and told each to fetch his instrument and climb on to the water-lily leaves and play a merry tune.

'Yes, Your Majesty!' they cried, and clambered quickly up. Then they struck up such a loud merry tune that all the fairies and sprites away by the dancing ring listened in astonishment. Then they all ran helter-skelter to the lake to see what the music could be.

There they found the queen, sitting on a water-lily, with the frogs playing their instruments as merrily as could be.

'Look! Look!' cried the fairies. 'The water lilies have brought their leaves to the surface!'

'What fun! What fun!' cried the water sprites, jumping on to the leaves. 'Oh, Your Majesty, we could dance on these! May we?'

'Yes, you may!' answered the queen, smiling. 'And now, whenever the fairies hold a dance in the fairy ring, *you* may hold a dance on the lily leaves, for the frogs will play for you until dawn!'

'Oh, thank you, thank you!' cried the sprites in great delight. They each took a partner and were soon gaily dancing on the smooth lily leaves, while the fairies looked on in wonder.

When dawn came nothing was to be seen of the queen or the fairies. The water sprites were gone, and so were the frogs and their instruments. But calm and steady the water-lily leaves floated on the water, waiting for the time when little feet should dance on them once again.

Look at them, next time you pass by a lake. The biggest leaf you see is the one that the queen sits on. Don't you think it was a splendid idea of hers?

The King's Hairbrush

The King's Hairbrush

ONCE UPON a time there was a king who had a wonderful hairbrush. His name was Rumbledy and he ruled over Ho-Ho Land, where the yellow pixies live. He had bought his hairbrush from the Moon-Witch, and people say that he paid her a hundred glittering diamonds for it.

The king had straight hair – very straight indeed, but as soon as he used the magic hairbrush, hey presto, his hair curled beautifully all over his head! Then how handsome he looked! His queen praised him and his courtiers rushed for their cameras at once. He certainly looked very nice.

Now the king didn't tell anyone, not even his queen, about his new hairbrush. Everyone thought his hair had suddenly turned curly, and they told him he was very lucky. The king kept his brush locked up in a drawer, and he only took it out once each twenty-four hours, and that was at ten o'clock at night, just before he went to bed.

He had to use his magic brush once each night, or his hair became as straight as ever. So he would sit on his bed and brush his hair ten times – and then he would know that his hair would be curly the next day for certain.

Now one night King Rumbledy quite forgot to draw the blinds before he sat own on the bed to brush his hair. He was tired that night, for he had been to a party, and it was almost midnight. The king never liked to stay out after midnight for at twelve o'clock his hair always went straight again. It lost its magic then.

Rumbledy yawned and took off his crown. He

slipped his arms out of his gold and silver coat and threw it on the bed. He could hear the queen splashing in her bath, so he thought he would take out his hairbrush from the locked drawer and brush his hair before she came to bed.

Just as he took it from his drawer, the big clock in the palace hall struck midnight. It said 'Dong' very loudly twelve times – and as the last stroke died away the king's hair lost its curls and became as straight as could be! How different he looked!

Now out in the palace garden was Longnose, a pixie, who was most inquisitive. He always wanted to poke his long nose into everything. He loved to peep through keyholes, he liked to look into everyone's windows, and he loved to find out secrets. He was a most unpleasant fellow.

Longnose was in the palace garden because he had seen a light in the king's bedroom, and had noticed that the blinds were not drawn. He had jumped over the palace wall, and had crept up underneath the window. Then he climbed up a tree whose branches tapped against the window and peeped into the bedroom to see what he could see.

'Perhaps I shall see if the king uses a gold toothbrush or not,' he said to himself. 'What a bit of news to tell my friends, if he does! Or perhaps I shall hear him snore.'

But what Longnose did see was far more exciting than anything he had thought of!

He saw King Rumbledy go to a drawer and take out a brush – and then Longnose suddenly noticed that the king's hair was straight – just as straight as could be, so that the king looked quite different. Then, when Rumbledy brushed his hair with the little yellow hairbrush, hey presto! His hair curled up again as tight as could be, and was perfectly lovely!

So that's how he gets his curls, thought Longnose. *Well, well! What a bit of news!*

The king popped the hairbrush down on a table by the window and bent to look at his hair in the glass.

Then a wicked thought came to Longnose. He slipped his hand in at the window, took up the hairbrush without the king seeing him, and hopped down the tree as fast as ever he could!

He ran down the palace garden and climbed over the wall as quick as lightning. Then off he went to his little cottage in the wood, holding the hairbrush tightly in his hand.

He lit a candle when he was safely inside the cottage. He looked carefully at the little yellow brush. It seemed quite ordinary – but it wasn't! Ah, Longnose knew what magic lay in that small brush!

He looked in the glass. His hair was straight and greasy. He would brush it well and let it grow curly like the king's. How good-looking he would be then!

So he brushed his hair with the magic hairbrush – and, hey presto, how his long hair curled! It bunched itself tightly round his head, and Longnose looked quite different. He was very pleased. He put the brush

345

down on a table and looked at himself with delight.

And then a queer thing happened. The yellow hairbrush suddenly jumped up from the table and rapped him hard on the knuckles! Then it leapt into the air and vanished! At least, Longnose *thought* it had vanished – it hadn't really. It had just flown up the chimney and stayed there, angry because someone had used it who had no business to.

Longnose looked for it and then gave it up. Most delighted with his curly hair, he got into bed and fell asleep. But in the night he awoke to feel something very queer happening to him. Something was gently brushing his long nose!

It was the brush. It had come down from the chimney and was brushing Longnose's nose. When it felt the pixie waking up, it fled back to the chimney again.

Longnose sneezed twice and fell asleep once more – but, oh, my goodness me, when he got up the next morning and looked in the glass, what did he see? The most peculiar-looking nose he had ever come across in his life!

It was curly! Yes, really. The brush had brushed it, and it had curled itself round like a corkscrew. Longnose looked very queer. His hair was curly too, but that looked all right. It was his nose that looked so dreadful.

'Oh, my goodness me!' cried Longnose in dismay. 'Look at my nose! Whatever am I to do? I can't possibly go out like this! Everyone will laugh at me.'

He tried to pull his nose straight, but he couldn't. It wouldn't go straight. It was as curly as could be. When he took out his handkerchief and blew his nose, it made a noise like a big trumpet. It was dreadful, and Longnose wept big tears for a whole hour.

He decided that he wouldn't go out that day, then nobody would see him. So, although the sun was shining beautifully, Longnose stayed indoors, hardly daring to look at himself in the glass. He wondered and wondered where the brush had gone to, but he never once thought of looking up the chimney.

He went to bed a very sad little pixie that night – and, oh, dear me, in the middle of the night the brush came down from its hiding place and woke Longnose up again! This time it brushed his long, pointed ears, and Longnose lay trembling in bed, not daring to move.

In the morning his ears had gone all curly! You should have seen them! They looked very queer. Longnose groaned when he saw them – and then he saw that his hair had gone straight again, for, you know, it needed to be brushed each night with the magic brush, if it was to keep curly. But his nose was still as curly as ever. The magic had stayed in that.

'How I wish I hadn't been so sly, peeping in at the king's window,' wept Longnose. 'It serves me right. But what am I to do? I can't keep indoors for ever. Besides, I shall soon have to go out shopping and get some things in to eat. I've hardly any bread left, and no butter at all.'

THE KING'S HAIRBRUSH

Now all this time the king had been wondering and wondering where his hairbrush had gone. He had hunted for it everywhere, and made the queen quite cross, because she didn't know what he was looking for, and he wouldn't tell her.

When the second night came and still there was no brush to be found, the king was most upset. He knew that his hair would be as straight as a poker the next day. But it wasn't a bit of good – he couldn't find that brush anywhere. And no wonder, because it was hiding safely up the chimney in Longnose's cottage!

The poor king couldn't keep his secret any longer. He awoke the next morning with his hair in long, straight tresses falling to his shoulders. He looked dreadful. He called the royal barber to him and commanded him to cut his hair short. The man stared in the greatest surprise at the king's straight hair. When he had finished cutting it he rushed out and told all his friends what he had done.

Then the king sent his heralds out, for he meant to

349

get his hairbrush back. They set out on horseback, blowing silver trumpets, and reading from big sheets of parchment.

'Oyez, oyez, the king offers a great reward to anyone who will return his lost yellow hairbrush, which has the power of making the hair curl. Oyez, Oyez!'

What a chattering there was all over the kingdom! How everyone hunted and searched! But nobody could find that brush.

Now there was a small pixie called Dumpling, who lived next door to Longnose. He was a kind-hearted little fellow, and when he didn't see Longnose coming out to shop, or running into his garden to hang up clothes, he wondered if he was ill.

So he went to knock at the door and ask Longnose.

'Go away,' said Longnose from indoors. 'I'm all right. Go away.'

Dumpling went away, but he couldn't help wondering why Longnose sounded so cross.

He must *be ill!* thought Dumpling. *Well, I'll just make him one of my famous raspberry jellies, and put it in at the kitchen window without a word. He can eat it if he wants to.*

So he made a jelly, and as soon as it was set, he crept into Longnose's back garden. He went to the kitchen window and peeped in, meaning to put the jelly on the table that stood just inside the window.

And, oh, dear, he saw Longnose sitting by the fire – but *was* it Longnose? *Could* it be Longnose? What a dreadful curly nose! And, oh, those awful curly ears! Whatever had happened? Dumpling gave a frightened shriek, dropped the jelly on to his toes, and fled away.

He went back to his own cottage and sat down to think – and suddenly he knew what had happened to poor Longnose. The naughty pixie had somehow got hold of the magic hairbrush, and by some mistake his nose and ears had become curly!

'Poor Longnose,' said Dumpling, shaking his head. 'No wonder he won't come out of doors. I will go to the king and tell him what I know, and maybe he will go to Longnose and make him say where the brush is, and cure his nose and ears.'

So he told King Rumbledy, and the king at once set out for Longnose's cottage. Rat-tat-tat! He knocked at the door, and then, without waiting for Longnose to say 'come in', he walked straight in!

The pixie jumped up in fright; when he saw the king before him he nearly fell flat with fear and astonishment.

'How did you get your curly nose and ears?' asked the king sternly.

Longnose began to stutter and stammer, and at last he told how he had peeped in at the king's window and seen him use the magic brush. The king listened to him with a frown.

Then he clapped his hands three times and said, 'Where are you, brush? Come out with a rush!'

At once the hairbrush rushed down the chimney and fell into the king's hand. How pleased he was to see it! He turned to go – but Longnose pulled at his arm.

'Your Majesty. What about *me*? Can you make my nose and ears straight again? Oh, please, please do!'

'Longnose,' said the king sternly, 'I have heard of you and your sly, interfering ways, always peeping and prying. 'I *could* make your nose and ears right again, but I'm not going to. They will get straight by themselves as soon as you get out of your horrid habits of peeping and prying – but if you forget and become deceitful again, you will find them becoming curly – so beware!'

Poor Longnose! He cried and cried when the king had gone. He *had* to go out shopping, and he didn't know what he would do when people pointed their fingers at him and laughed.

But he had to put up with it. It was all his own fault.

'I'll never, never poke my nose into other people's business again!' vowed Longnose. 'This has been a terrible lesson to me!'

So he stopped peeping and prying into other people's affairs – and gradually his nose became straight again, and his ears lost their curliness. He is nearly all right now, so I expect in the end he will become quite a nice fellow.

Dumpling got the reward, which was half a sack of gold. He bought a cow, a sheep and a goat, and he is very happy looking after them. The king brushes his hair once more each night with the magic hairbrush, and now his hair is as curly as ever, so *he*'s quite happy too. *I'd* like to use that brush just once, wouldn't you?

Goldilocks and the
Three Bears

Goldilocks and the Three Bears

ONCE UPON a time there was a little girl called Goldilocks. She lived with her father and mother in a little cottage at the edge of a wood. Her hair was so long and so golden that everyone called her Goldilocks, and even her mother had forgotten what her proper name was.

Goldilocks used to play in the fields and woods all day long and pick blackberries when they were ripe and primroses and bluebells when they were in bloom.

'You can play anywhere you like,' said her father, 'but, Goldilocks, you *must not* follow any little path that goes deep into the woods.'

'Why not?' asked Goldilocks.

'Because,' said her father, 'deep in the woods live the three bears in their cottage and they may catch you if you go near them.'

'Three bears in a cottage!' said Goldilocks in astonishment. 'Daddy, what fun! *Do* let me go and visit.'

'Don't be so silly,' said her mother sharply. 'They'll eat you.'

'Oh, but, Mummy,' said Goldilocks, 'I *would* like to see bears that live in a cottage just like us. Do they clean the front door knocker and wash the front doorsteps, just like we do?'

'If you ask any more silly questions,' said her mother, 'I'll send you to bed. And mind, Goldilocks, do what Daddy says, and *don't* go following any little paths into the heart of the woods.'

Well, of course, Goldilocks thought and thought and thought about the three bears who lived in a cottage, and the more she thought about them, the more she wanted to see them. She was not at all an obedient little girl, and at last she made up her mind that she really *must* go and see the three bears.

I won't go at a time when they are likely to be about, she thought, *just in case they might eat me. I shouldn't like that at all. Now when shall I go?*

Goldilocks was closely watched by her father and mother, for they knew she was disobedient. She found it very difficult to go exploring in the woods to find the little path that the bears used.

'I shall get up very, *very* early in the morning,' she decided at last, 'when Mummy and Daddy are asleep, and then go and spy on the three bears. *They'll* be asleep too, so I shan't come to any harm at all. And won't it be fun to say I went and saw the three bears in the wood? Everybody will think I am *very* brave!'

So the next morning, when the larks were singing and the sun was sending long, slanting rays through the trees, Goldilocks got up and dressed herself. She slipped out of the cottage door and ran into the woods, skipping and dancing as she went along.

'Where's the little path, where's the little path?' she sang.

And then she suddenly found it. It was the dearest, tiniest path she had ever seen, and it seemed to invite her to run along it. It wound here and there, as green as could be, and was bordered each side by wild strawberry plants, whose little red strawberries gleamed red in the sunlight.

Goldilocks didn't stop for those, though; she was much too anxious to get to the bears' cottage. She ran along, most excited and happy. The path wound in and out through the trees, and then at last ran right up to the little white gate.

On the gate was painted BEAR COTTAGE. It led to a little cottage rather like Goldilocks's, only much smaller. She stared at it in delight.

I wonder – I do wonder – if the bears are at home, she thought. *I'll peep and see.*

She tiptoed up to the front door, which was open, and looked in. No one was about at all. Goldilocks pushed the door right open and walked in.

'I expect I'm the first little girl who's ever called on the three bears,' she said to herself as she looked round.

She was tired after her long walk, and looked for a chair to sit down on. There were three – one very big, one not so big, and one very small.

'Father Bear's, Mother Bear's and Little Bear's,' said Goldilocks as she saw the three chairs. 'I'll try Father Bear's.'

She sat down in the great armchair.

'Oh my!' she cried, jumping up again. 'It's much, much too big! I'll try Mother Bear's chair.'

She sat down in Mother Bear's chair but she didn't like that either.

'It's so hard!' she said. 'It ought to have a cushion. I'll try Little Bear's.'

She sat down on Little Bear's chair. It fitted her perfectly, and was as soft and as cosy as could be.

'This is *lovely*!' said Goldilocks, settling herself well down into it.

Then crack! It broke, and down went Goldilocks on the floor.

'Oh, dear!' she said. 'What a nuisance! I do hope Little Bear won't be cross!'

Then she caught sight of the table. It was laid for breakfast. On it were three bowls of steaming porridge, one very big, one not so big, and one very small.

'Oh, the bears have porridge!' cried Goldilocks in delight. 'I didn't know bears ate porridge. I wonder what it tastes like?'

She took up a spoon and tasted Father Bear's porridge.

'Oh!' she cried. 'It's too hot! It's burnt my tongue. I'll try Mother Bear's.'

She put her spoon into Mother Bear's porridge and tasted that – but she didn't like it at all.

'It's not sweet,' she said. 'I don't like it. I'll try Little Bear's.'

She tasted Little Bear's porridge, and that had treacle on, and was as nice as could be.

'What *lovely* porridge!' cried Goldilocks. 'I must have another taste!'

She went on tasting it until it was all gone!

When she had finished she looked around the room, and saw stairs leading upwards.

'I wonder if there's a bedroom,' she said. 'Do bears sleep in beds? I *would* like to know!'

She ran up the stairs, and came to a tidy little bedroom with three beds in it. One was very big, one not so big, and one very small.

'I'll try Father Bear's,' said Goldilocks, and climbed up on it. She lay down, but she didn't like it at all.

'It's *much* too hard!' she said, and climbed down again.

Then she tried Mother Bear's bed, but she didn't like that either.

'It's *much* too soft,' she said. 'I'll try Little Bear's.'

She climbed up on the Little Bear's bed and snuggled down.

'Oh, it's lovely!' she said. 'It's cosy and warm, and

just big enough for me!'

She put her head down on the pillow, and what do you think – she fell fast asleep! There she was in the three bears' cottage, sleeping soundly on Little Bear's bed! It was really a very silly thing to do.

Now all this time the three bears had been out for a walk to let their porridge cool. After a while they came back, wiped their feet, and stepped indoors. Then Father Bear suddenly saw that his chair had been sat in.

'Who's been sitting in *my* chair?' he growled angrily.

'And who's been sitting in *my* chair?' cried Mother Bear.

'And who's been sitting in *my* chair, and broken it?' squeaked Little Bear sadly.

Then Father Bear looked at the table and saw that his porridge had been tasted.

'Who's been tasting *my* porridge?' he growled crossly.

'And who's been tasting *my* porridge?' said Mother Bear.

'And who's been tasting *my* porridge, and eaten it all up?' squeaked Little Bear, crying.

The three bears couldn't understand it.

'Let's go upstairs and see if anything has been touched there!' said Father Bear.

So up they went. The first thing Father Bear saw was his bed, all crumpled and crushed.

'Who's been lying on *my* bed?' he growled.

'And who's been lying on *my* bed?' growled Mother Bear.

'And who's been lying on *my* bed, and is sleeping there *now*?' squeaked Little Bear in the greatest excitement.

All at once Goldilocks awoke, and saw the three bears staring at her in angry surprise. She was dreadfully frightened and jumped out of bed at once. The bears made a grab at her, and just missed her. Down the stairs she fled as fast as ever she could go, with all the bears lumbering after her.

'*I'll* catch her!' cried Father Bear.

'*I'll* catch her!' cried Mother Bear.

'*I'll* catch her and eat her like she's eaten my porridge!' squeaked Little Bear, tumbling over the mat.

But they didn't catch her. She was too quick for them, and ran panting down the path and into the woods faster than she had ever run in her life before!

Soon she had left the bears behind, and, after a long while, she reached her home again.

'I'll never, *never*, *never* be disobedient again!' she sobbed, when she told her father and mother all about her adventure.

But they scolded her and sent her to bed for the rest of the day just to make sure – and you'll be glad to hear that she never was disobedient again, but grew up into quite a nice little girl.

As for the three bears, nobody knows what became of them. They moved away, and were never heard of again.

The Artful Pixie

The Artful Pixie

ONCE UPON a time the people of Heyho Land were in a very bad way, because two powerful people lived there – a Wumple Witch and a Whistling Wizard. The witch lived down in the plains, and frightened all the people there, and the wizard lived up in the hills, and scared the shepherds a dozen times a week.

So you see, it wasn't a bit of good moving to get away from the witch because then the people lived too near the wizard; or if they moved away from the wizard, they came across the witch. It was all most upsetting.

If only the Wumple Witch and the Whistling

Wizard had kept to their own work, and left the people of Heyho alone, it would have been all right. But they didn't leave them alone. They were always borrowing their black cats to help them to make spells, or stealing their broomsticks to fly about on, or even making the people themselves work for them.

One day the Wumple Witch made a mistake in one of her spells, which was to make a saucepan that would boil without a fire beneath it; and because of the mistake every single saucepan in the land jumped off the stove and ran off to goodness knows where. Anyhow, they were never seen again, and that made the people of Heyho very angry.

Then the very next week the wizard played a trick on everyone just for fun. He whistled for the wind, and whispered something in his ear – and in a trice the wind went off and flicked away everybody's hat! It brought them all to the wizard and laid them down in a neat row at his feet.

The people didn't dare to complain, but they were

most annoyed. It meant that everyone had to go and buy a new hat, and as the Whistling Wizard owned the only hat shop in the town, he made quite a lot of money out of his trick.

'What can we do to get rid of the Wumple Witch and the Whistling Wizard?' groaned the people when they met one another in the street. 'Let's have a secret meeting about it.'

So they did – but not even the wisest of them could think of a really safe way to get rid of them. Everyone was too much afraid. And then a small pixie, called Kiki, got up and spoke.

'I believe I have an idea,' he said in his high, little voice. '*We* can't get rid of the witch and the wizard – but why not let them get rid of each other?'

'It *sounds* very clever,' said Bron, the head brownie. 'But how can it be done? You are full of ideas, Kiki, but they are not much good when we try to carry them out!'

'All right!' said Kiki, offended. 'I'll do the idea

myself! I won't tell you anything about it! But what will you give me if I manage to get rid of the Wumple Witch and the Whistling Wizard? Tell me that!'

Bron, the brownie, didn't believe that the sharp-eyed little pixie would do anything very clever, so he laughed and said, 'Oh, you shall be king of Heyho, if you *do* manage to get rid of those two nuisances – but you won't!'

Kiki's eyes grew very bright. He skipped out of the meeting hall and went to his tiny cottage. It was very bare and shabby, for Kiki was poor. But soon he would be rich! He would be king of Heyho! He would have a carriage and a pair of horses! Oho! Wouldn't everyone stare at him?

He sat down on a three-legged stool and thought hard. Then he took up his bag of tools, put on his leather apron and set off to the castle in the plain where lived the powerful Wumple Witch. Kiki was a carpenter by trade, and he often went round the countryside offering to mend things for people – a broken chair, a shelf and things like that.

Now he went to the Wumple Witch. He knocked boldly on the door of the castle, and the big black cat, who was the chief servant of the witch, opened the door to him.

'I'm Kiki the carpenter,' said the pixie. 'Any jobs want doing, sir? I can mend anything that's made of wood!'

The black cat was so delighted at being called 'sir', that he bade Kiki come in. 'Yes,' he said, 'there's many jobs want doing in this place. It's hard to get a carpenter in, for they're all afraid of the witch, and *she* is too busy to bother about mending things that break!'

Kiki went in and set to work on a dozen broken things. He put a new leg on a table; he put up two shelves in the kitchen; he made a new door for a cupboard. He worked so quickly and so well that the black cat spoke to the Wumple Witch about him.

'Your Highness,' said the cat to the Witch, 'there's a clever little fellow here, mending things in the kitchen. Would you like him to mend your magic wand for you – the one that broke in half when you hit me with it? And what about your biggest broomstick? That could do with mending too, I think, because it's getting old and soon won't bear us both when we go flying on it at night.'

'All right, bring him in, and I'll tell him what I want done,' said the witch. This was just what Kiki wanted. He skipped into the witch's strange workroom, which was full of green smoke, and bowed to her.

'I want you to mend that and that,' said the witch, pointing to the wand and the broomstick.

'I'm sorry,' said Kiki. 'I haven't time to stop. I've to go and mend for someone else tomorrow.'

'Oh!' said the Witch, frowning in a most terrifying manner. 'And who is more important than I am, I should like to know?'

'The Whistling Wizard, up in the hills,' said Kiki at once. 'He's much cleverer than you are. He can do heaps of things you can't do. Oh, he's a wonderful fellow, and everyone thinks so!'

The Wumple Witch looked as black as thunder.

'Well, you tell the Whistling Wizard *this*!' she said angrily. 'You tell him that if he likes I'll meet him somewhere and show him how much cleverer I am than *he* is! Ho, ho! *I'll* show him a few things! And when I've shown him a little of what I can do, I'll send him whistling away to the moon!'

'But could you really do that?' asked Kiki, pretending to be most surprised. 'I don't believe you!'

'Oh, don't you?' said the Witch. 'Well, wait and see, that's all! Now go to the Wizard – and just tell him my message!'

Kiki went. He rode on a rabbit all the way to the hills, and the next morning he knocked on the Whistling Wizard's castle door. A grey goose opened it, the Wizard's latest servant. When she heard that Kiki could mend anything made of wood she bade him come in.

Soon he was busy mending chairs and cupboards.

The wizard passed him by one day and watched him.

'It's a pity you weren't here last week,' he said. 'I had a magic candlestick that wanted mending, and you could have done it well.'

'I couldn't have come last week,' said Kiki, going on with his work. 'I was working for somebody very important.'

'Oh, indeed!' said the Wizard snappily. 'And who is more important than I am, I should like to know?'

'Why, the Wumple Witch of course!' said Kiki. 'She's very clever and very powerful – much more powerful than *you* are, Whistling Wizard!'

'What nonsense!' said the Wizard angrily. 'Why, I could beat her at anything she liked to mention!'

'Oh, no, you couldn't!' said Kiki, hammering a nail into a chair leg. 'Oh, no! The Wumple Witch doesn't think much of *you*! She sent you a message to say she'll meet you any time you like, and show you what a stupid fellow you are compared with her! And, what's more, she'll send you whistling away to the moon when she's finished with you!'

The wizard was so tremendously astonished that for two whole minutes he really couldn't say a word. He just stood there, swallowing and gulping with rage.

Kiki looked at him. 'Don't be frightened,' he said, pretending that he thought the wizard was terrified. 'I'll see she doesn't really hurt you! I don't expect she'll send you whistling to the moon unless you annoy her.'

Well! The wizard simply exploded with rage! You should have seen him! He went red in the face, and then purple, and then black! Kiki felt rather frightened but he didn't show it. He just went on hammering.

'You go and tell the Wumple Witch I'll meet her in the Cowslip Meadow at twelve o'clock on Tuesday morning,' he shouted. 'And I'll show her a few things! Yes, I will! I'll send her down to the middle of the earth before I've done with her!'

Kiki gathered up his tools and ran off. He was overjoyed because his plan seemed to be working so well. By the next morning he was knocking at the Wumple Witch's door, and the black cat let him in, quite pleased to see him.

'I've a message for the Wumple Witch,' said Kiki, and he went to see her.

'Madam,' he said. 'I come from the Whistling Wizard. He laughs to think that you believe yourself to be more powerful than he is! He will meet you at twelve o'clock on Tuesday morning in Cowslip Meadow, and there he will show you how clever he is and how foolish *you* are! And to end with he'll send you off to the middle of the earth!'

The Wumple Witch shook so much with anger that her hat fell off. She picked it up and put it on again.

'I'll be there!' she said. 'I'll be there!'

And she *was* there, exactly as the clock struck twelve on Tuesday morning. The Whistling Wizard was there too – and so was the grey goose, his servant. The witch's black cat was there as well, making up his mind to eat the goose if he had a chance. And all the people of Heyho Land were there – but not too near, for sparks flew and flames shot up when witches and wizards quarrelled!

Well, the wonderful things they did! You should have seen them! The wizard made a plum tree grow, and it grew so high that it touched the sky. The plums on it were as big as melons. Then he waved his stick and the plums changed to gold! It was marvellous.

The witch said that was a silly trick, one she had learnt when she was three years old. She made a tall tower grow out of the ground, and suddenly it arched over and changed into a fierce dragon which was just going to eat the wizard's grey goose when the witch laughed and made it disappear in smoke.

'Pooh!' said the wizard. 'A simple trick! Can you do nothing better than that?'

Ah, then they really got going! They changed themselves into lions and ogres, they made the thunder sound in the sky, and they caught the lightning and lit candles with it. They cut pieces out of the clouds and made themselves purple and grey cloaks. And all the time they were watching for a chance to throw a spell on each other, for they were fiercely jealous of one another's power.

The watching people were frightened to see such magic. They wished they hadn't come. Only Kiki was delighted, for he felt sure that it would all end right.

Suddenly there was a pause in the magic. Neither witch nor wizard could think of anything more to do for the moment – and in that minute they weaved spells upon each other! The Wizard whispered a powerful fly-away spell to send the Witch to the middle of the earth – and the Witch murmured a marvellous fly-away spell to send the Wizard up to the moon!

They each guessed what the other was doing – but it was too late! Before the wizard could stop himself he found that he was racing up through the air, off to the moon. And before the witch could stop *herself*, she was sinking down, down, down to the very middle of the earth.

They were gone! Yes, they were gone! The Whistling Wizard was only a speck in the sky, and soon he had disappeared altogether. The ground closed over the Wumple Witch, and there was no sign of her either.

'They've gone, they've gone, they've gone!' cried all the people in excitement, and they clapped their hands for joy.

'Yes, and they won't come back!' said Kiki, feeling very grand. '*I* did it! *I* planned it all!'

'How?' cried everyone. 'How?'

Then Kiki told them everything: and how they praised him and patted him on the back!

'You deserve to be our king!' they cried. 'You do really! Come along and we'll crown you this very day.'

So they crowned him king, and he had a carriage and pair, a palace, and as much as he liked to eat, which pleased him very much. He made a very good king, and was always fair and just.

As for the Whistling Wizard and the Wumple Witch, they were prisoners for ever. Some say that the Man in the Moon is no other than the wizard – and others say that when there is an earthquake it's just the Wumple Witch twisting and turning in the middle of the earth, trying her hardest to get free. But I really don't know about that.

Dick Whittington

Dick Whittington

THERE WAS once a poor boy called Dick Whittington who tramped to London to get work. With him went his great friend, a tabby cat. When Dick got to London he found that work was very difficult to get, but at last he got a place as a kitchen boy. His cat lived in the scullery and Dick gave her half of his food.

The cook was very unkind to Dick. She often scolded him, but, worst of all, so Dick thought, she snapped at his friend, the tabby cat.

At last one day Dick thought he really couldn't put up with such ill-treatment any longer. Besides, Puss was sad, and he really couldn't stand that.

'We'll go away,' he cried. 'Come, Puss!'

Together they set out early one morning, and soon left London behind. When he had walked a good way Dick felt tired, and sat down. He had nothing to eat, and his heart was sad.

'What shall we do, Puss?' he said. 'We are very unlucky, you and I!'

Just at that minute the bells of London began to ring, and, to Dick's astonishment, they seemed to be ringing a message to him:

Turn again, Whittington,

Lord Mayor of London Town,

Turn again, Whittington,

Lord Mayor of London Town!'

So they seemed to say, and Dick jumped up.

'Come, Puss!' he cried. 'We'll go back and try again! I'll never be mayor, but I'll be something nearly as good, if only I work hard.'

So back they went, and to Dick's astonishment he found that the bad-tempered cook had left that very morning! He *was* glad he had gone back!

The new cook was kind to him, and told his master what a clever, willing boy Dick was. Soon his master took notice of him, and his master's daughter smiled at him. Dick thought she was as beautiful as the day.

One morning the master called all his servants in to him.

'I am sending out a ship to trade in the east,' he said. 'Have any of you anything to give to my captain? He may be able to bring you silks and jewels in return!'

The servants pressed eagerly round the captain and begged him to buy them what he could with their money for they knew that a pound in foreign countries would buy far more than a pound in London.

'What about you, Dick?' asked his master.

'I haven't any money, or anything I could sell,' said Dick.

'Send your tabby cat!' laughed the servants.

'Yes, send her for luck,' whispered his master's daughter to him.

So he gave his cat to the captain, and begged him to take care of her.

The ship set sail and came to a faraway land. The captain went to dine with the king and found him sighing in despair because of a great plague of mice.

'Look at them!' he cried. 'They are everywhere! In my bed, in my soup, even in my clothes! I would give a bag of gold to be rid of them!'

Suddenly the captain thought of Dick's cat. He fetched her and set her down. Immediately she dashed at the mice, and in one minute had killed nearly a hundred!

'What a marvellous creature!' cried the king, who had never before come across a cat. 'Will you sell her to me?'

'No, I will lend her to you while I am here,' said the captain, 'if you will give me three bags of gold!'

The king gave them to him, and then settled down to watch the wonderful cat killing all the mice.

To the captain's delight Puss had four kittens while she was there. The king said he would give a bag of gold for each, if the captain would leave them in his kingdom to grow up into cats.

The captain promised, and soon after that sailed away with Puss and seven fine bags of gold. When he got to London he called for Dick, and told him what he had done.

'Seven bags of gold!' cried Dick in wonder. 'Why, I am a rich man! Dear old Puss, what a lot of money you have earned for me!'

He kissed the cat and went to find his master.

'I am rich now,' he said. 'Will you let me marry your daughter? She loves me, and I love her.'

His master was only too pleased, for Dick had grown up into a splendid young man. He gave his daughter to him, and they were married.

Sometime after, Dick was made Lord Mayor of

London. How proud he was and how everyone loved him and his wife for their goodness to the poor.

And when he was made Lord Mayor the bells rang loudly, and said:

'Welcome, Dick Whittington,
Lord Mayor of London Town,
Welcome Dick Whittington,
Lord Mayor of London Town!'

Acknowledgements

All efforts have been made to seek necessary permissions.

The stories in this publication first appeared in the following publications:

'Mr Wumble and the Dragon' first appeared in *Sunny Stories for Little Folks*, No. 44, 1928.

'Cinderella' first appeared in *Sunny Stories for Little Folks*, No. 1, 1926.

'He Didn't Believe in Fairies' first appeared in *Sunny Stories for Little Folks*, No. 179, 1933.

'The Sleeping Beauty' first appeared in *Sunny Stories for Little Folks*, No. 1, 1926.

'The Lucky Fairy' first appeared in *Sunny Stories for Little Folks*, No. 47, 1928.

'Puss in Boots' first appeared in *Sunny Stories for Little Folks*, No. 7, 1926.

'Oriell's Mistake' first appeared in *The Teachers World*, No. 972, 1923.

'The Story of Rumpelstiltskin' first appeared in *Sunny Stories for Little Folks*, No. 7, 1926.

'The Land of Golden Things' first appeared in *Sunny Stories for Little Folks*, No. 82, 1929.

'The Hardy Tin Soldier' first appeared in *Sunny Stories for Little Folks*, No. 23, 1927.

'The Strange Tale of the Unicorn' first appeared in *Sunny Stories for Little Folks*, No. 142, 1932.

'The Odd Little Bird' first appeared in *Sunny Stories for Little Folks*, No. 190, 1934.

'The Enchanted Sword' first appeared in *The Knights of the Round Table*, published by George Newnes in 1930.

'A Lovely Welcome Home' first appeared in *Merry Moments*, No. 183, 1922.

'Little Red Riding Hood' first appeared as 'Red Riding Hood' in *Fairy Tales for the Little Ones*, published by Birn Brothers in 1924.

ACKNOWLEDGEMENTS

'The Dragon Called Snap' first appeared in *The Teachers World*, No. 1621, 1934.

'The Biscuit Tree' first appeared in *Enid Blyton's Sunny Stories*, No. 231, 1941.

'Mister Fee-Fie-Fo' first appeared in *Sunny Stories for Little Folks*, No. 150, 1932.

'Rapunzel' first appeared in *Sunny Stories for Little Folks*, No. 21, 1927.

'The Princess and the Red Goblin' first appeared in *Sunny Stories for Little Folks*, No. 26, 1927.

'The Tooth Under the Pillow' first appeared in *Enid Blyton's Sunny Stories*, No. 285, 1942.

'Beauty and the Beast' first appeared in *Sunny Stories for Little Folks*, No. 7, 1926.

'Old Mother Wrinkle' first appeared in *Enid Blyton's Sunny Stories*, No. 75, 1938.

'The Four-Leaved Clover' first appeared in *Enid Blyton's Sunny Stories*, No. 484, 1950.

'The Imp Without a Name' first appeared in *Enid Blyton's Sunny Stories*, No. 73, 1938.

'The Disappointed Sprites' first appeared in *The Teacher's Treasury*, Vol. 1, 1926.

'The King's Hairbrush' first appeared in *Sunny Stories for Little Folks*, No. 177, 1933.

'Goldilocks and the Three Bears' first appeared as 'Goldenhair and the Three Bears' in *Sunny Stories for Little Folks*, No. 1, 1926.

'The Artful Pixie' first appeared in *Sunny Stories for Little Folks*, No. 181, 1934.

'Dick Whittington' first appeared in *Sunny Stories for Little Folks*, No. 1, 1926.